"See? We're just alike, me and you,"

Gopher said with satisfaction. "Right?"

"Yeah," Buck said slowly, frowning. He stared into the mirror at the two sets of similar blue eyes. He reached out and scooped off some of the shaving cream along the little boy's chin. Rounded, not like his own angular chin, but with that haunting sense of familiarity he hadn't been able to pin down.

Crazy, the thought that had flashed through his mind.

Impossible.

Reason argued that he was letting his imagination run away with him. Reason told him that what he suspected couldn't possibly be true. He *knew* Gopher could not be *his* son. But his heart looked in the mirror and told him something else, told him that the impossible could, sometimes, be *possible*. And wouldn't the heart recognize the truth?

Jessie's son.

His?

Dear Reader,

Happy Valentine's Day! Silhouette Romance's Valentine to you is our special lineup this month, starting with *Daddy by Decision* by bestselling, award-winning author Lindsay Longford. When rugged cowboy Buck Riley sees his estranged ex with a child who looks just like him, he believes the little boy is his son. True or not, that belief in his heart—and his love for mother and child—is all he needs to be a FABULOUS FATHER.

And we're celebrating love and marriage with I'M YOUR GROOM, a five-book promotion about five irresistible heroes who say "I do" for a lifetime of love. In Carolyn Zane's *It's Raining Grooms,* a preacher's daughter prays for a husband and suddenly finds herself engaged to her gorgeous childhood nemesis. *To Wed Again?* by DeAnna Talcott tells the story of a divorced couple who are blessed with a second chance at marriage when they become instant parents. Next, in Judith Janeway's *An Accidental Marriage,* the maid of honor and the best man are forced to act like the eloped newlyweds when the bride's parents arrive!

Plus, two authors sure to become favorites make their Romance debuts this month. In *Husband Next Door* by Anne Ha, a very confirmed bachelor is reformed into marriage material, and in *Wedding Rings and Baby Things* by Teresa Southwick, an any-minute mom-to-be says "I do" to a marriage of convenience that leads to a lifetime of love....

I hope you enjoy all six of these wonderful books.

Warm wishes,

Melissa Senate,
Senior Editor
Silhouette Books

Please address questions and book requests to:
Silhouette Reader Service
U.S.: 3010 Walden Ave., P.O. Box 1325, Buffalo, NY 14269
Canadian: P.O. Box 609, Fort Erie, Ont. L2A 5X3

DADDY BY DECISION

Lindsay Longford

Silhouette
ROMANCE™
Published by Silhouette Books
America's Publisher of Contemporary Romance

 SILHOUETTE BOOKS

ISBN 0-373-19204-5

DADDY BY DECISION

Books by Lindsay Longford

Silhouette Romance

Jake's Child #696
Pete's Dragon #854
Annie and the Wise Men #977
The Cowboy, the Baby and the Runaway Bride #1073
The Cowboy and the Princess #1115
Undercover Daddy #1168
Daddy by Decision #1204

Silhouette Intimate Moments

Cade Boudreau's Revenge #390
Sullivan's Miracle #526

Silhouette Shadows

Lover in the Shadows #29
Dark Moon #53

LINDSAY LONGFORD,

like most writers, is a reader. She even reads toothpaste labels in desperation! A former high school English teacher with an M.A. in literature, she began writing romance novels because she wanted to create stories that touched readers' emotions by transporting them to a world where good things happened to good people and happily-ever-after is possible with a little work.

Her first book, *Jake's Child,* was nominated for Best New Series Author, Best Silhouette Romance and received a Special Achievement Award for Best First Series Book from *Romantic Times.* It was also a finalist for the Romance Writers of America RITA Award for Best First Book. Her Silhouette Romance title *Annie and the Wise Men* won the RITA for the best Traditional Romance of 1993.

Dear George—I mean, Gopher,

I know you've found it a little strange to have me hanging around lately. You're used to having your momma all to yourself, and all of a sudden, here I am, barging in.

I surely do appreciate your concern. Fact is, it makes me feel better that your momma has such a strong and stalwart—that means really brave—guy taking care of her.

Your momma seems to think that my hanging around with you both is some form of midlife crisis. That means—oh, to heck with what that means. Here's what's important: I would never, ever hurt you or your momma. I solemnly swear it, on fish bones and lizard guts and everything that's brave and true.

Maybe someday, you and your momma will find your castle big enough for three. Until then, I shall remain your loyal subject—

Jonas "Buck" Riley
a.k.a. "Sir Cowboy"

Chapter One

It was all those damned weddings.

Since the second wedding in the Tyler family, Buck had been as itchy and cranky as a bull stomping and snorting in the pasture. Shoot, who'd have expected ol' easygoing I'm-a-rambling-man Hank, the baby of the family, to waltz Jilly Elliott off to the altar in the wake of T.J. and Callie's wedding?

And all those kids running around! A man couldn't take two steps without tripping over Gracie or Charlie or Hank's fifteen-month-old twin terrors, Duke and Gorp. And Hank couldn't stop patting Jilly's swollen belly where Flynn-to-be waited to make his appearance.

Buck picked up a package of crackers and a jar of cheese glop, scowling at the boxes of baby diapers stacked in front of him. Babies! Hell, Hank and T.J. were repopulating the whole damned county all on their own. He stared for a moment at the carton. The pink-cheeked infant's smile was goofily appealing, the sparkle in the chocolate brown eyes— He stopped his thoughts.

Gritting his teeth, Buck shoved his sweat-stained hat back on his head. Who was he kidding? What he needed couldn't be found in an all-night convenience mart. He sighed and scratched at the mosquito bite on the back of his neck.

Hell of a note to find himself feeling like an outsider in his own family. He thought he'd gotten over that sense of being on the other side of the fence a long time ago, but there was nothing like a long night alone to bring back all those old feelings, that bottomless pit of loneliness welling inside and pulling him into its emptiness. He rubbed his bristly chin irritably. Maybe what ailed him was nothing more than the full moon making him restless and dissatisfied with his life, with himself.

He'd never missed one of his mother's birthday parties, and he wouldn't have missed this one, not really, not even with this blue funk settling over him. But still—

An elbow jostled him. "Sorry," a husky voice muttered. Caught by the scent of flowers and cinnamon, he glanced up, welcoming the escape from his thoughts, but the woman had vanished behind a towering stack of jars of salsa, leaving behind her only a light fragrance and the memory of that low, soft bedroom voice.

Buck slapped the jar of cheese spread back on the shelf and glared at the bright fluorescence of the Palmetto Mart's nighttime world.

He'd been a fool to leave the shabby isolation of his motel room. Nothing in that motel room to distract him, that was the problem, and he couldn't stand staring at that two-bit painting of some pink and green tropical landscape one more second. In the face of those Pepto-Bismol pinks and puke greens, the Palmetto Mart had seemed like an oasis.

"Frankie? Where did you hide the chunky peanut butter?" The husky voice rasped again along Buck's raw nerve endings, a wet-dog shiver of a reaction.

"Moved it, Miz McDonald. Next aisle over." Frankie's voice cracked on the last word.

"Thanks. You're a lifesaver." Shoes squeaked against the floor, punctuating the low voice.

Turning into the adjacent aisle as Frankie spoke, Buck saw a slim back and nicely rounded tush moving slowly down the aisle in front of him. And a very nice little tush it was, he decided, gratefully looking away from bright-eyed baby faces to study the slow sway of those curves under paint-spattered cutoffs. The frayed ends dangled against smooth, tanned thighs that curved down to sturdy calves and narrow feet in ragged sneakers and neon purple socks.

Buck blinked. Maybe it was the Palmetto Mart's lighting. Nope. At second glance, the socks were still blindingly purple. With small black and green race cars stitched into the sides. His gaze lifted to the slim, soft arm reaching for a bottle of orange Gatorade on the top shelf. With a quick stride he closed the space between him and the owner of the sweetest tush he'd seen in years. And then, too, there was that quite remarkable voice that slithered along his skin. Maybe the Palmetto had more possibilities than he'd imagined.

Leaning against the display, one arm balanced along the top, he gestured to the shelf. "Need a helping hand?"

"What I *need* is to be taller. Or, absent that miracle, I could use a stepladder," she said with a self-mocking lift of her shoulder. She started to turn toward him and then went very still, her head dipping down.

"No ladders around. Just me."

"I can manage," she said in a cool little voice. Three-quarters turned away from him, her face averted, she stared at the blue basket holding a loaf of bread and a shrink-wrapped miniature car. Streaky brown hair straggled loose from a scraped-back ponytail. Obscuring his view of her face, curly tendrils flopped, floated, and coiled with her jerky movements. Wild hair, warm brown and gold, the kind that made a man want to twine its strands around his fingers, stroke its silkiness and bury his face in its softness.

Devilment and the long night stretching emptily in front of him loosened his tongue. Honesty made him admit to himself that maybe, too, he wanted to get a rise out of her after her cool dismissal. So, stretching out the syllables and slouching in the best Clint Eastwood tradition, he drawled, "No problem, little missy."

Her shoulders tightened, nothing more than a movement

under her white shirt, and he wondered if "little missy" was going to stomp on his boots. Diverted, he didn't move, merely waited to see what she would do.

Not looking at him, she stretched on tiptoe and tilted the bottle next to the one he held. "As I said, cowboy, I'll manage."

Cowboy? Intrigued, he straightened. Little missy had a razor-edged tongue. He had an urge to upend a broom, pull out a bit of straw and stick it into his mouth. Or find a chaw of tobacco. Anything to complete the image. With a fair degree of effort, he managed to kill the urge to thicken his drawl into molasses, but he couldn't resist the impulse to tweak her. "Like *I* said, sugar, no problem."

Grabbing the bottle with a small, square hand, she snubbed him with four throaty syllables. "Thanks, but no thanks."

A peculiar sense of familiarity tugged at his memory and killed the teasing. Frowning, he leaned toward her. "Pardon me, ma'am, but—"

Slipping around the corner of the aisle, she disappeared behind a cardboard drop of Fourth of July sparklers and American flags. Brushed by her hip, one of the flags stirred, moved in the breeze of her passing, then collapsed among the red, white and blues.

Well, damn. Startled by the swiftness of her departure, Buck blinked again.

Her message was real, real clear. A sensible man would have picked up his corn puffs and his beer and hit the road. Buck meant to leave. Hell, he knew that's exactly what he should do. But he wasn't quite ready to face Maxie's Tropical Motel, and, anyway, something about that throaty voice kept nudging him in her direction.

So he wasn't a sensible man. What else was new?

Watching her progression through the Palmetto Mart in the silvered metal camera in a corner overhead, he ambled back past the cheese spread and crackers, past the diapers and jars of creamed this and pureed that until he reached the middle of the aisle nearest the door and the checkout counter.

Face-to-face with a row of very personal feminine products,

he paused and shrugged. Probably not the best spot for him to linger. He moved back down the aisle toward the shelf of roasted, sugared and peppered peanuts. With one eye on the camera's black-and-white screen and the twitch of little missy's gray denim, he fumbled for a jar of salted pecans and stuffed it on top of the six-pack under his arm. Manly-man stuff, all right. Cowboy stuff.

Strolling toward the counter, he stepped behind her, waiting patiently as she unloaded peanut butter, white bread, milk, Gatorade and the toy car. Holding herself stiffly, she angled against him, away from him, her narrow shoulders hunched forward, protectively. In the TV screen above them, Buck saw the grainy gray blur of her downcast face.

Frowning, he narrowed his eyes and studied the screen while that scent of cinnamon and pulse-beat warm skin beguiled him.

"You're gonna need a dollar and fifty-eight cents more. Or you could put something back."

"Drat." Gold and brown strands of hair trembled as she dug into her patchwork quilt purse. "I left in a big old hurry, Frankie." She heaved wallet, daybook and three paperbacks onto the counter. "Fiddle, I can't even find my checkbook. Phooey."

The skinny teenager behind the counter lifted his shoulders. "Sorry, Miz McDonald, I'd loan you a couple of dollars, but I'm broke." His grin was sheepish. "Me and Eva went out last night."

"Ah, I see. Big date, huh?" A rawhide dog bone joined the stack on the counter. As Buck watched the monitor, she looked up at Frankie and a smile flashed across the screen. In that second Buck had a clear view of a square face with a stubborn jawline, a wide, generous mouth and enormous eyes behind round, metal-framed glasses. The screen blurred again as she scrabbled through her bottomless purse once more, dumping tissues, wads of paper and a yellow squirt gun onto the counter this time.

"Here." Buck lifted the pistol and carefully placed a five-dollar bill under it. ''No reason to hold up the joint. Keep the change.'' He thought she'd look his way.

She didn't. She fingered the jar of peanut butter, brushed the milk jug with a knuckle, and slid the racing car off to the side. ''Ring my order up, please, Frankie, without the toy.'' She nudged the bill along the counter, back toward Buck. ''Not necessary. But thanks. Again.'' The chilliness crisping the edges of her warmed-brandy voice was unmistakable.

Even rejecting him, she didn't turn his way, not even a sidelong glance. Buck's curiosity was killing him. He wanted to see her face up close, not in the grayness of the monitor. He had a hankering to see if the face matched the voice. If he could see her face, he could quiet that nagging familiarity.

But Frankie bagged her purchases with surprising efficiency, and she was out the door, leaving behind her a tantalizing scent of cinnamon on the humid night air circling into the Palmetto Mart.

''Hang on, Frankie. I'll be back.'' Buck shoved his beer and peanuts to the side, strode to the door and caught it before it swung closed.

Outside, damp air pressed against his skin, filled his lungs with heavy wetness. The air smelled of earth and kerosene from a distant plane. Low on the horizon, the golden moon cast fitful shadows across the concrete. He didn't see the woman who'd intrigued him out of his funk, but headlights from a dark van suddenly switched on, blinding him, and he glimpsed a silhouette in the driver's seat.

He knew it was the woman from the Palmetto. The engine idled, as if she were waiting, like him, indecisive, and Buck stood there, staring into the darkness of the van, his attention focused on that small shape behind the windshield. The lights from her van bridged the moonlit darkness between them, connected them in a curiously intimate way.

Brassy darkness and silence.

Heat rising from the dark pavement, the smell of cinnamon and jasmine floating on the wet air.

And the two of them at each end of that path of light, his blood pounding in his ears.

Shielding his eyes, Buck strained to see through the shimmering whiteness of the car lights. He needed to see her. Holding his hand up, he walked slowly toward her, from the darkness at the Palmetto's exit into the lights of her van. Slowly, slowly, both hands hanging to his sides now, he walked toward her, blinded.

"So long, cowboy!"

The tinge of satisfaction in the throaty voice stopped him. Puzzled, he shoved his hat farther back on his head. As he did, the van reversed, smoothly turning toward the frontage road and the entrance to the highway. The left-turn signal winked triumphantly at him.

He could have loped across the parking lot and intercepted the car at the stoplight. But that edge of intimate hostility in her actions held him in place, thinking, as the light changed and the van turned left toward town.

She hadn't been afraid of him. He knew that because she'd waited, watching him, even as he approached her. No, it wasn't fear of him that caused her prickly wariness. Something altogether different. A kind of amused taunting, as if she'd proven something to herself.

"Well, well, well." Shoving his hands into his jeans pockets, he watched until the red lights vanished into the hot darkness.

And then he smiled.

In the moments when his eyes adjusted back to darkness before she'd turned onto the frontage road, he'd seen the van's license plate. Gopher 1. Not a license plate he'd be apt to forget.

Back in the Palmetto Mart, Frankie's scowled warning greeted him. "I was watching you, mister. I'd a called the cops if you bothered Miz McDonald."

"Good for you, Frankie," Buck said gently, defusing the bristling animosity radiating from the spindly boy. "That was exactly the right thing to do. You did good."

"Sorry if I was rude, man," Frankie muttered, checking prices, "but I didn't know what you was up to. And I wasn't gonna let you hurt her."

"That wasn't my intention." Buck handed over a twenty, took his change.

"It's late. I didn't know what you had in mind."

Buck laughed. "To tell you the truth, Frankie, I don't know what I had in mind, either. I was—interested, that's all. Miz McDonald is an interesting woman."

Frankie's face reddened. "Yeah. She's nice."

"I'm sure she is. I could tell." Buck watched Frankie's face turn a brighter shade of beet.

"Yeah, well, I'm the night manager, and my customers are my responsibility. I take care of Miz McDonald when she comes in."

Buck recognized the signs of a teenage crush when he saw one. Hell, he'd lived through T.J. and Hank's frequent throes of love. Then T.J. met Callie Jo, and everything changed for both his brothers. Buck had always had his suspicions about Hank's feelings toward Callie Jo, but Hank, the most open man in the world, could keep his own counsel when he wanted. Anyway, Hank worshiped Jilly and their kids, so the past was the past.

In the meantime, the bantam across from him was scratching for a showdown. Shoot, the kid wouldn't break a hundred and thirty pounds, but his heart was in the right place. Buck tried not to smile. The kid didn't deserve that.

"Nobody's going to mess with her while I'm here." Frankie squared narrow shoulders defiantly and tried to stare Buck down.

Looking away, casually, easily, he gave Frankie the move, letting the kid save face, the same way he'd yielded to the heat of his younger brothers when they'd been on the brink of manhood. "She's lucky you're in charge, Frankie. I could tell she likes your store. I'll bet she comes here a lot?"

Frankie nodded.

"She must feel safe. With you around, watching out for her. And for the rest of your customers." Sticking a finger through the plastic loops of the six-pack, Buck smiled, tipped his hat with a finger, and strolled toward the door. "Nice meetin' you, Frankie. Take care now, hear?"

"Sure thing, man." Frankie held his shoulders so far back Buck could have clipped them together with a clothespin.

Kids. Sheesh. Buck stepped outside into the steamy night. Rolling his head back and forth, he considered his choices. Maxie's in town? Out to T.J.'s ranch? Or get in the Jeep and haul rear half the night south, back to Okeechobee and his own ranch and groves?

The road, glistening black under the low-lying moon, stretched in front of him. Truth was, he had nowhere he wanted to go, nothing pulling at him, no one to help him while away the lonely night hours. A light breeze tugged at his hat, filtered through the straw brim, brushed against his cheek like a feathery kiss. Scraps of paper on the concrete lifted, stirred, floated to his feet. One was a receipt from the Palmetto. He reached down to pick it up. *Eggs, vanilla ice cream, milk.*

Not hers.

He crushed the receipt between his fingers, holding it for a moment, staring off into the thick, empty night.

Impulse and the memory of red lights winking off toward town made him about-face back into the Palmetto.

Jessie's hands were slippery with sweat on the plastic steering wheel. Even with the windows of the van down and the wind whipping in, perspiration pooled along her spine, slid to the waistband of her shorts. Skeezix, her shaggy mutt of undetermined origins with the temperament of an angel, eased up from the back. Sidling in next to her, he stuck his nose out her window. "Come on, you big lug. Scoot over to your own side, will you?" She pushed at the dog until he moved over and stuck his head out the passenger window.

She wondered if Jonas Buckminster Riley had recognized her in spite of her careful attempts not to look his way. Even though he'd always been shrewd and fast on the uptake, a lot had changed in the last five years, most of all her.

He hadn't recognized her. He would have said something if he had. But maybe not. A complicated man, he liked playing games. Tiny shivers slipped over her skin. And in her innermost soul, she knew it wasn't fear running through her. The frisson skipping along her nerve endings was a remnant of another life, another Jessie, not this Jessie barreling down the highway in a van filled with the smell of dogs and take-out hamburger. She'd left that other Jessie behind, a long time ago.

As she unwrapped the cold hamburger and nudged it toward the dog, Skeezix moaned happily and pulled his head inside. She sneezed as dog hair drifted toward her. "Good dog! But you silly fool, why didn't you eat it when it was hot?" She rubbed the dog's head and scratched behind his ears. Slopping paper and hamburger bits over the seat, Skeezix collapsed onto her thighs with a wiggle of contentment. "Guess who I ran into tonight, Skeez?" Skeezix wiggled closer, his tongue lapping wetly against her cutoffs. "A ghost from my past, and you didn't even let out a howl? For shame. Some dog you are. Would you have defended me if I'd needed you, you big mutt?" Skeezix rolled his head and thumped his heavy tail a couple of times. "Oh, sure, that's what you say now. But where were you ten minutes ago, buster?"

She was glad her ghost hadn't remembered her. Of course she was.

But.

"So long, cowboy!" The sound of her last words lingered in her ears. Surely she hadn't wanted him to stop her with a flood of for-old-times'-sake memories? Had she?

But, her unruly tongue running ahead of her brain, she'd called out, "So long, cowboy!" Had that been a note of challenge, of "gotcha" in her voice? Had she wanted him to recognize her? Had some deep perversity ruled her in that last second? Surely not.

But she'd called out. In that last, crucial second, she'd called out to him.

In the light from her headlights, he'd looked bigger, tougher. A little mean with his eyes narrowed like that, a little baffled but thinking hard as he'd stared back at her from the darkness. Even sitting yards apart from him, she'd felt the insistent beating of his will against her, his determination to solve the puzzle she represented to him. That insatiable curiosity, that inability to turn away from an unanswered question—that quality had made him a brilliant lawyer.

He'd been fearsome, his cross-examinations stripping away evasions until a witness sat as vulnerable as a deer caught in the cross hairs, waiting. And then Jonas Buckminster Riley would deliver the killing blow, gently, cleanly, so elegantly that the witness seemed almost to welcome the coup de grace that put finish to the relentless, unending questions delivered in Jonas's chillingly polite drawl.

No, the Palmetto Mart cowboy in the cream-colored straw cowboy hat and scruffy jeans might be as curious as ever, but he was not the man she remembered. Long, rangy muscles and sloping shoulders replaced the reed-thin frame she'd known; that thin, hard body covered by suits so expensively sumptuous that one time, driven by some crazy impulse as she'd passed in back of him, she'd stroked the baby-soft fabric of a jacket left casually hanging on the back of his chair.

He'd known, of course. He'd looked up at her in that moment when her index finger glided against the sleeve, slipped inside to the lining still warm from his body, and lingered against the silk.

"You like that, huh?" he'd asked and smiled, his brilliant blue eyes blazing her into ashes.

Lifting one eyebrow, she'd run her finger carelessly over the lining. "A bit too uptown for me. But then clothes make the man, so they say." Brushing her hands together, knowing he was watching her every twitch and movement, she'd walked away, into her own office, her heart slamming against her ribs with each step.

"Do they really? Say that?" His whispery drawl had tickled the hairs along the back of her neck, sent goose bumps down her arms, her chest. "And what do you say, Ms. Bell?" His smile turned edgy, his narrowed gaze assessing, as he swiveled his chair toward her and focused all his fierce intelligence on her, pinning her in the searing beam of his gaze.

She'd smiled in return, lifted one eyebrow, and shut her door, leaving his question unanswered.

She wasn't that Jessica Bell anymore. That woman seemed

alien to her now. If she were different now, so, too, must he be. Inside. Outside. They weren't the same people at all. So why was her heart still pumping so hard she felt as if she'd run a race? What possible impact on her life could a chance encounter at the Palmetto Mart mean at this point in her life?

Diddly. That's what.

She braked the car in the driveway. Home. Hers. One she'd bought and paid for by herself. Downstairs in the family room a solitary splash of blue-white from the television broke the thickness of the night. Skeezix lumbered out behind her, woofing and circling her, weaving in and out between her legs until she laid her hand on top of his head. "Quiet, dopey. You want to wake up the whole neighborhood?" Two different canine greetings answered Skeezix.

The front door opened. A tiny silhouette in the rectangle of the doorjamb tilted his head and scrubbed at his eyes. "Hey," he said sleepily.

"Hey yourself, sugar." She swung him up over Skeezix and into her arms. "It's mighty late. Why aren't you asleep?"

"Me and Aunt Lolly waited for you. But we was hungry, so we ate all the pizza. Ev'ry last bite." He spread his arms wide and clasped her around the neck, his chubby bare arms tight against her. "Loofah chewed the cheese off the cardboard."

"Bad dog."

"She was hungry, too."

"I guess that's okay, then." Jessie nuzzled the warm, sweaty neck of her son. "C'mon, sugar, let's say good night to Auntie Lolly and get you to bed."

"'Kay." His soft hair tickled her nose as he leaned against her and fixed her with eyes as blue as her own. "But I am not at all tired."

"No?"

"Nope. Not sleepy *at all*."

Jessie stumbled against Skeezix, who'd crowded in behind her as she closed the door. Gopher tilted over her arm and blew a kiss at the dog. "Night, Skeezes. Sleep tight." Her son glanced shrewdly up at her. "Skeezes isn't sleepy. Me and Skeezes'll sleep better together, right?"

Laughing, Jessie scrunched him to her. "Is that so, sugar-doll?"

"Yep," he said with satisfaction as his head drooped against her breast and his thumb found its way to his small mouth. "That's so."

Waiting inside the arch to the family room, her neighbor and honorary aunt Lolly rolled her eyes. "He did take a long nap. But he's been going nonstop since he woke up. Can you give me some of whatever you're feeding him? So I can keep up?" Her bony freckled face was cheerfully rueful. "We've dug worms, we've walked the dogs, we've made brownies. And taken three baths. Lord love a duck, Jessie, how do you keep up with him?"

"Practice." Jessie anchored Gopher higher on one shoulder and slid open her desk drawer, reaching inside for her checkbook. "Hang on for a minute while I carry him up to bed, will you? And then I'll write you a check if that's okay?"

"You don't have to pay me, Jess. I told you, I love staying with Gopher. Anyway, what else do I have to do most nights?"

"Take the check, Lolly. It's better this way. Your time's valuable, too, you know, no matter what you choose to do with it." With her hip balancing the weight of her son and one arm curled around his rear, Jessie scribbled on a check. If she didn't, Lolly would be gone before Jessie could come back downstairs. "And who knows? One of these nights you might decide to go out and do something wild and crazy."

"Oh, sure," Lolly scoffed, her face crumpling into soft folds of humor. "You seen any gents looking for sixty-two-year-old dates?"

"Sure, but you can go out with a guy for company. Doesn't have to be a date." Jessie shifted Gopher and handed Lolly the check. "And you have friends. You could go to the movies. Or to the theater over in Sarasota? Lolly, listen. Life's too short to pull up the drawbridge and hide out forever. You've got a lot of years ahead of you. Enjoy them. Go out. Party. Even if the wildest you get is going to the DeSoto Salad Bar.''

"Maybe.'' Lolly opened the door.

With Lolly, "maybe'' meant "no way.''

Lolly stuffed the check inside her vinyl purse. "Jess, I'll take Loofah and Mitzi home with me. You can pick them up tomorrow if you're going to use them at the rehab center.''

"Right. I'll come get them. I wanted to give Skeezix the day off. Loofah and Mitzi work really well. They're sweethearts. The patients are crazy about them.'' Jessie blew Lolly a kiss and headed up the stairs, Gopher murmuring in her ear all the way.

"I *luuv* Lolly. And I *luuuv* Skeezes and I love my mommy and Loofah—''

"I know, sugar, and I *luuuv* you.'' She kissed his soft cheek where a red scratch testified to his busy day. "Let's tuck you in bed and you can tell me all about your day.'' Pulling back the faded purple dinosaur sheets, Jessie slid him under the light cover and shucked off her sneakers, climbing in beside him. "Oof, sugar, you're getting so big.''

"That's my job,'' he told her sleepily. "Going to Sunny Days Early Learning Preschool, and coloring and getting big. I *luuuv* Sunny Days.'' He wriggled his rump into the curve of her arm and waist.

Curling him close to her, his tough little body radiating heat, Jessie shut her eyes wearily. "So how many worms did you collect for our fishing trip tomorrow, sugar?''

"Maybe seventy-leven zillion.'' He half rose and kissed the underneath side of her chin, a sweet, damp press of not-quite-baby mouth that never failed to squeeze her heart.

"That should do the trick,'' she said, hugging him tightly to her, this child, a child she'd never expected, hadn't wanted yet would die for. Smoothing his hair off his forehead, she returned his kiss. *Her* child.

But it was Jonas Buckminster's intense eyes she saw in the darkness as she drifted into sleep beside her son.

Sometime before dawn the phone rang in the stuffy room

f Maxie's Motel, dragging Buck out of a fitful sleep where
e'd been running and running and running, chasing some-
hing, someone, the figure disappearing into shadows and mist.
n the dream where an iron band squeezed his heart, he'd
needed to stop that figure, ask it—what? Something. He
yawned. Sheets twisted around his naked body, wound in be-
ween his legs. Groggy, mouth dry, he fumbled for the phone,
ifting it to his ear.

His brother T.J. spoke, the words fast and harsh. "Daddy's
n the hospital, Buck."

He sat up, pulling free of sweaty sheets. "What? You're
kidding. He was fine today at Mama's birthday party."

T.J. paused, and Buck heard the unspoken words in the
ension in T.J.'s voice. "I don't know. No one's said anything
et. I don't know what happened, but Mama wants you here.
Can you come?"

"Yeah. I'll be there in half an hour."

Static crackled between them. "Good thing you stayed over,
Buck."

"Yeah." There was nothing more to be said.

Hanging up the phone, Buck rubbed his eyes. Hoyt? In the
hospital? There must be a mistake. Tough, as strong as the
oak tree on the Tyler ranch that now belonged to T.J., Hoyt
was immortal. A man among men, the patriarch of patriarchs.
John Wayne and Clint Eastwood couldn't walk in his shadow.

Shrugging into jeans, Buck zipped and snapped with steady
fingers while the air conditioner labored in the muggy air.
Hoyt was going to be fine. Nothing else was possible. Jamming loose change into one pocket and his wallet into the
threadbare rear pocket, Buck scanned the shadows of the
room.

Funny, but he'd almost decided to drive back down to
Okeechobee last night. Instead he'd stayed and checked the
listings for McDonalds in the Tarpon City phone book. Too
many to call, so he'd tossed the book on the floor and crawled
into bed.

If he hadn't stayed, he would have been out in the pasture,
too far away to make it back to Tarpon City before late eve-

ning. Fate. Shaking his head, he grabbed the Jeep keys from the round table near the window.

On the scarred and peeling veneer of the bed stand, the toy car glittered in the predawn watery light, gold flecks sparkling in its bright red metal.

A quick flash of memory stilled him. The keys dangled from his slack fingers.

Her head bent away from him, that streaky hair curling and sliding every which way, she'd hesitated, her hand lingering on the toy. And, briefly glimpsed in the monitor, her square chinned face with its wide mouth.

Like mist on the bayou, memory swirled gently through his brain. Picking up the toy, he frowned as he touched the smooth, sleek finish.

Chapter Two

Buck shut the door to his room and jogged to the Jeep through the dim parking lot where gray shadows lingered under cabbage palms and moss-draped oaks. Even before sunrise, heat radiated up from the black asphalt and thickened the humid air.

Twenty minutes later, he slammed through the automatic doors of the hospital and leaned over the fake plastic wood of the reception desk. "Hoyt Tyler? Room?"

Before the woman with the elaborate cornrow hairstyle could answer, a deep voice interrupted. "Hey, Buck. How many red lights did you run? Or did you scam a police escort?" Thomas Jefferson Tyler, Buck's middle brother, punched him on the shoulder and draped an arm across Buck's shoulders as he guided him to the bank of elevators. "You look like ten miles of bad highway."

"How's Daddy?" Buck wiped the back of his hand across his forehead. The expression in T.J.'s eyes unnerved him.

"Don't know. He's in intensive care. Internal bleeding, apparently. Anyway," T.J. said, punching the Up button, "they're running tests, Mama looks like hell, and the doctors aren't saying anything. I'm just real glad the folks are here and not back in Seattle.''

"Yeah." Studying his brother's tightly controlled expression, Buck felt his stomach tighten. T.J. didn't panic. Like all the Tylers, like Hoyt himself, T.J. was the calm in the center of the hurricane. But at the moment T.J. vibrated with clamped-down feelings, that unspoken urgency communicating itself to Buck, screeching at him like fingernails on a blackboard. "Can I see Daddy?"

"Sure. Every hour they let someone in for five minutes, but don't expect much. I think they have him doped up. Hank and Mama are in the waiting room. Callie and Jilly are coming up later. They're switching off with the kids and looking after the ranch. Everybody's staying there until we find out what's going on. You going to come on out and bunk with us?"

"Don't think so."

Watching the red lights blink at each stop, they rode up to the seventh floor in silence. Jamming his hands into his pockets, Buck turned off his whirling thoughts, let himself exist in the cocoon of metal and piped-in music. He found himself closing his fist around the miniature car he'd stuffed into his pocket at the last minute. Fingering its smooth surface like a prayer stone, he traced its unseen shape over and over.

In the intensive care waiting room, his mother sat waiting, her hands folded tightly together, her face gray-white. "I'm glad T.J. got hold of you. Hank's with Hoyt. We brought him in ourselves. The ambulance would have taken too long." Her voice was steady, her smile a brave slash of pink, but she didn't unclasp her trembling hands.

Hugging her and covering her hands with his much larger ones, Buck held her close to him. He didn't expect her to collapse in tears. Bea Tyler wouldn't. She did her crying in private. But her clasped hands trembled with a fine vibration that belied her outward calm and he felt helpless to comfort her. He folded himself into a sitting position next to her. "What happened?"

As his mother talked, sorting through her thoughts, her words slow and halting, Buck greeted Hank, his younger brother, with a nod. Stricken, all his sunshine good humor vanished, Hank seemed suddenly years older than he had the day before, reminding Buck of T.J. when he heard about his infant son's diabetes.

A word here, a question there, thoughts sputtering into speech and trailing off, they finally abandoned the attempt and sat in silence, together but alone, while the clock moved sluggishly through the unending minutes until it was Buck's turn to visit.

Entering the quiet room filled with the electrical whirring of IV pumps and flashing green monitors, Buck stopped. Tubes went down Hoyt's mouth, nose, draped across the bed. Two bags of packed cells for blood transfusion hung on a pole beside the bed. As Buck stayed at the entrance, his hand on the curtain, Hoyt opened his eyes and glanced around.

Walking around the foot of the bed, Buck smiled. "Hey, Daddy. You gave us a hell of a scare."

Hoyt's gaze lit briefly on Buck before his eyelids drooped shut, closing Buck out.

Buck felt as though he'd been punched in the gut. He'd heard what his mama and brothers had told him, but even so, they hadn't prepared him. Reality transcended words.

The only father he'd ever known had looked at him and not recognized him. Loss, enormous and incomprehensible, swamped him.

With his hand gripping Hoyt's, Buck swallowed. Cast adrift, he clung to the weathered, rough hand of the man who'd raised him, who'd taught him everything, and it was the longest, loneliest five minutes of his life.

Five minutes at a time, the day crept into late afternoon.

Buck felt the walls of the waiting room closing in on him, imprisoning him with each passing moment until he thought he'd throw something at the picture on the wall.

He'd volunteered to come back and spend the night at the hospital so that the others could go back to the ranch. Callie Jo and Jilly were coming for the evening, but then they would return home so that everyone could rest and regroup while he stayed guard. He convinced everyone that was the best plan. They all had family responsibilities. He didn't.

In the meantime, it was going to be another three hours before he could see Hoyt again, and he seriously didn't think he could take three more minutes penned up in the waiting room. He jerked to his feet. "I need a change of scenery. Some fresh air. Maybe a walk."

Hank, T.J. and their mother looked up at him, their eyes as dazed as his must be. Maybe it was the way they all stared at him with the same blue-green gaze, maybe it was the restlessness that had settled in his bones some time past, but he felt like a kid on the other side of a fence. "I'm going down for coffee. Y'all want some? A sandwich? Mama, can't I get you something?"

One after the other, like dominoes falling, they shook their heads. Once more he was struck by his brothers' similarities to their mother and to Hoyt. And today more than ever before, Buck felt like the cuckoo in the robin's nest.

He passed up the cafeteria, opting for the more private vending machine lounge. Leaning his arm against the cold drink machine, he rested his forehead on his arm, staring uncomprehendingly at the selections. The machine *ka-chunked* as he pressed the round red button. A can of cola rolled to the bottom. All he could see was Hoyt's blank gaze staring at him and looking away.

Hoyt was only sixty-one. In the prime of life, he could still ride and rope with the best of them. Buck shut his eyes. Anger and frustration boiling up in him, he wanted to slam his fist into the machine.

He wanted to grab Hoyt out of that bed, rip all the tubes and machines off him and run hell-for-leather out of the damned hospital. Get Hoyt out into the fresh air at the ranch where he belonged.

But for the second time in his life, he was helpless.

And so he stayed there, breathing deeply, trying to block out all the anger and fury ripping through him. He wasn't used to being helpless, and he didn't like it one damned bit.

It was a faint, elusive scent that alerted him, a hint of cinnamon underlying flowers.

He lifted his head and stared straight into eyes as bright blue as his own, eyes that widened before going carefully blank behind round glasses that slipped down her narrow nose.

The black-and-white reflection in the Palmetto Mart monitor had been way, way off the mark—only a shadow of the real woman. In living color, her wide mouth didn't need bright lipstick. Rosy pink and full, her lips curved deeply into small creases at the corners, a mouth made for laughing, for kissing. Falling to her shoulders in a mass of gold and brown, curls twisted into small corkscrews and tendrils.

She was wearing some kind of loose green-blue dress with tiny, silly straps over a sleeveless white T-shirt, and the light ocean-colored material swirled around her bare legs as she stepped sideways, away from him. The dollar bill fluttered in her hand as she moved.

"We meet again, Miz McDonald." Pushing away from the drink machine, he scooped up his can of cola and nodded once to her. He gestured with the can toward her dollar and watched those curves around her lips tighten as pink tinged the edges of apple cheeks. "Flush—and flushed today, I see."

Her fingers clutching her dollar, her wallet-on-a-string drooping down her arm, Jessie wondered how fate could be so wicked. "Hmm," she said and turned, walking steadily to the coffee machine, Jonas Buckminster Riley's long shadow covering her as he followed.

"What brings you to Tarpon City Memorial Hospital?" His drawl curled around the question, putting a slight spin on it that made her wary.

"Now why would I tell *you?*" Jessie smiled sweetly at him and marched toward the coffee machine, her heart thumping sickeningly. She knew how Jonas could move panther-smooth from one unimportant question into a killing pounce.

"Ah, answering a question with a question. You're either Irish or a lawyer."

She didn't stumble, didn't stop, didn't flinch. "And you can't stop fishing, can yóu? Maybe the cowboy getup," she said, gesturing toward his jeans and shirt, "is only camouflage, and you're the lawyer?" She pleated her dollar. Had she gone too far? Drat her tongue.

"You didn't answer my question." He braced himself against the soup vending machine.

"No, I didn't, did I?" Again Jessie managed her teeth-on-edge-sweet smile. "How perceptive of you. To catch that. Oooh, I'm so impressed." She batted her eyelashes mockingly.

She thought the sound she heard coming from him was a surprised snort. It might have been a cough. She hoped it was a cough.

"Once in a while I'm—perceptive," he said with not an ounce of inflection in his melted caramel drawl.

Her mind ran through every possibility she could think of. He knew. He remembered. He didn't remember anything and was simply on the prowl.

Except that Jonas never prowled. He'd never needed to. She believed he must have learned in his cradle that all things came to him who waited, because everything did come to Jonas, sooner or later. He'd never had to exert himself for attention. He'd been the man with the golden touch, the man everyone crowded around while he backed away from the attention.

And the more elusive he became, the more sought after he was.

"Cat got your tongue, Miz McDonald?" Moving from the machine, he settled himself comfortably against the wall and popped the top of the can, holding her gaze the entire time as he tipped the can back and drank from it. Beneath the mischief in his eyes, she saw the veiled curiosity, the interest that sharpened with each second she didn't answer. "You surprise me." Again there was a note of another meaning rippling beneath his comment.

Sun and age lines radiated from the corners of his eyes. Caught in the power of that gaze, breathless and dizzy, Jessie couldn't look away. She felt as though he were willing her to answer him, to tell him everything he wanted to know, to wring her soul dry.

The artificial light of the lounge highlighted deep mahogany gleams in his thick hair, glimmered in the red-gold bristles that darkened his narrow, hard-angled face. Lowering the can, he hooked his thumb in the waistband of his jeans. As he shifted, the washed-thin fabric pulled across his flat belly and tightened against his thighs.

Jonas Riley had been born to wear tight, worn jeans.

Jessie's dollar drifted to the floor, brushed her leg and broke the spell he'd spun. Her face burning, she stooped to pick up the bill, took a toe-deep breath and stood up. Turning away from him with a quick movement, she pressed her fist into her skirt.

He didn't remember her.

But he was on the hunt.

Feeding the dollar into the coffee machine with shaking fingers, she tapped the coffee selections without even seeing what she was choosing.

"Don't you want to know how I know your name, Miz McDonald?" He hadn't moved, but his question shivered the hairs on the back of her neck. "I'd think you'd be—interested. Me being a stranger and all?"

In the metal and plastic of the machine, she saw his rangy reflection. He was studying her, frowning, definitely on the hunt. "Don't you want to know, Miz McDonald? Aren't you a little curious?"

Goaded, she whirled, her skirt whipping around her. "I don't have to ask. I know. You were right behind me. You heard Frankie." Coffee slopped onto the floor.

"So I did." He closed the distance between them with one step and dropped a stack of napkins over the coffee stain at her feet. Squatting to swipe up the liquid, he glanced up at her, the light spilling over his face and throwing into sharp relief lines of strain and exhaustion she hadn't noticed earlier. "Well, Miz McDonald, you might want to remind your friend Frankie that it's not a good idea, even in a small town like Tarpon City, to identify his customers, especially his—" he glanced at her naked left hand "—single female ones." Soft and deceptively gentle, his voice drifted through the air, moved over her skin like a teasing feather stroke.

The Jonas she remembered was toying with her, seeking the weak spot. She knew it, and she still struck back, the old Jessie rising to the bait.

"Thanks for the helpful hint, cowboy. I'll make sure I mention your advice to Frankie."

Not fooling her one bit with his nonchalance, he pitched the wet brown wad of paper in the trash, took a final pull of his cola and asked, "By the way, does Miz McDonald have a first name?"

"And wouldn't she be a fool for telling you?" Jessie smiled sweetly. "Even with this being such a small town. And you the picture of respectability? It's a wonder I don't just hand you my safe-deposit number and key. Gosh, can't *imagine* why I don't." Quirking one eyebrow, she sipped deliberately from her plastic-coated cup, relaxed, all easy confidence, her voice as mellow as his as she continued. "And since you've been so helpful, may I return the favor, cowboy?"

"Of course, ma'am." He dropped the cola can into the recycling bin. "I'm always grateful for good advice." Butter-smooth, his polite tone matched the respectful tip of his head. But his eyes narrowed suddenly, as if she'd somehow made a mistake. Suddenly intent, he looked as if she'd handed him the end of the thread leading through the puzzle maze. "What was it you wanted to say?" He stepped back, waving her through as she approached the door.

Turning her head to look at him over her shoulder, she smiled. "Not much. Except that even cowboys go in for a shave and a change of clothes once in a while. Maybe you're working too hard at creating an image?"

She heard the quick intake of his breath. "Ah. I see. Clothes. The image. Yes, Miz McDonald, I sure do appreciate your input." Rich satisfaction rippled through his voice, over his face, as he smiled. "You've been right helpful, ma'am."

Jessie fled. She couldn't imagine what she'd revealed, but in giving in to her desire to score one tiny point off him, she'd obviously messed up somehow.

Fast-walking down the corridor to the parking lot, Jessie muttered under her breath. "Coffee. That was the problem. It wouldn't have killed me to skip my mocha latte for once." She should never have stopped in for coffee before leaving for home. But she always did. "Why would I expect to see Jonas Riley stretched out over the cola machine like some martyred saint?" Swearing at herself under her breath, she stomped down the hall.

For her, the road to hell was clearly paved with coffee beans.

Two nurses stared at her as she stormed by them, and then their eyes drifted past her, their steps slowed, and one of the nurses lifted a hand to fluff out shiny black hair.

Jessie fought the impulse to break into a flat-out run. She didn't have to look. Like the sun at high noon in summer, heat and determination came from the man keeping easy pace a step behind her.

"You took off in such a hurry, Miz McDonald, that you left your purse on the table near the door." Lean brown fingers dangled her wallet-on-a-string in front of her. "You're a busy lady, I reckon, rushing around the way you do, forgetting your wallet today, your checkbook last night?"

"I manage to fill my days," she muttered, reaching for the wallet.

"I'm sure you do." With a flick of his hand, he looped the burgundy leather strap over her neck. "Glad to help, ma'am," he added, his voice cordial, his manner solicitous, his cowboy act perfect down to the slightest tone and gesture.

But she'd observed Jonas Buckminster Riley in action, had seen the man who'd been a shark in court, urbane, cultivated, as he cut through bloody waters, and she didn't trust this blue-eyed, tough-featured cowboy metamorphosis any farther than she could pitch an elephant. "Yes, well, for the umpteenth time, thank you." She jerked as he touched her shoulder.

"Anything else I can do for you?" He straightened the strap, his knuckle sliding against her bare arm.

Prickles of alarm and awareness ran down her arm. She caught her breath. It was nothing more than a *touch*, nothing to be upset about, but her skin went hot and she wanted to shut her eyes and let him run that callused knuckle down her neck, across her shoulder—

Too many nights alone had made her forget the power of a simple touch.

Worse, she'd forgotten her susceptibility to the touch of Jonas Riley.

Clamping her arm close to her side, Jessie kept her gaze on the corridor floor, on the square, dusty toes of his boots. He'd had long, narrow, beautiful feet.

"Better?" He adjusted the strap once more, his face coming into her view as he stooped to her eye level, his breath mingling with her own, warm, cola-and-coffee-scented.

She'd known coffee would be her downfall. She hadn't expected it to tempt her in this manner, though. "Thank you. You're an exceptionally—*helpful*—person, aren't you?" Trying to outpace him, Jessie lengthened her stride, taking two and a half to every one of his and feeling crowded the whole time, surrounded by him, his energy, his sheer, overwhelming *presence.* "Or perhaps you're a retro Boy Scout?"

"I like to be useful."

"Good for you," Jessie said through gritted teeth. "The world could use a lot more useful men." She reached the automatic exit doors that swung open as she stepped toward them.

Huddled under the portico, the smokers cleared way for her. For Jonas. Hurrying toward her car, she fumbled for her keys, pulling them out. A wave of heat curled toward her from the concrete sidewalks, washed over her. The red sun lay fat and hot on the horizon and she wanted to be home, to escape the very solid spirit from her past. Just as she opened her van door, he stopped her.

"Wait." His hand closed around her elbow, his thumb flat against the inner pulse, and her heartbeat slammed in a staccato rhythm to that light, insistent pressure. His thumb was rough as he moved it against her skin, against her underarm in a slow, unconscious stroking that had nothing at all to do with the questions gleaming at her from his eyes.

"Take your hand off me, cowboy. Now."

Buck did.

She hadn't needed to tell him. As he'd touched her, her face had turned pinched and tight, and he'd already taken a step away from her. He recognized the desperation blazing in her eyes. Holding his hands up, palms toward her, he didn't move. "Sorry, Ms. McDonald. I wasn't thinking. I didn't mean to scare you."

"You didn't. I don't scare that easily." Not looking in back of her, she opened her van door and stepped quickly inside, shutting the door between them with a quiet snick. She stabbed the key into the ignition as she said in a low, furious voice, "But I don't like strange men grabbing me, cowboy, no matter how charming they are. And you don't know me well enough to be anything else except a stranger." Sunlight burnished her hair to pale gold.

Like an overlay, another image superimposed itself, this one in vivid color.

Her hair should have been sleek—a smooth, bright blond helmet cut close to her face, that full mouth dark red, seductive.

"But we've met before, haven't we?" Trying to meld the two images, he rested his hand on the open window of the van. A strand of her hair brushed the back of his hand, curled around his palm with the feel of a forgotten touch, a remembered kiss. "I know you, don't I?"

She looked as if he'd struck her. Her face went paper-white, and a rumbling growl came from the shadowy interior of the van. "Believe me, you don't know me at all." As she spoke, a wide head with enormous teeth and lolling tongue appeared next to hers at the window edge.

Buck kept his hand on the window. "Does he bite?"

"*She*. Yes, she does." Color was flowing slowly back into the woman's face as she regained her equilibrium.

"Bites, huh?" Buck scanned the dog's face, noting the wagging tail. "She doesn't strike me as a dog who'd bite." Dog slobber dripped on his hand but he didn't move, didn't try to pat that wide, rough head.

"Well, she does. Enthusiastically. Every chance she gets."

"Now why don't I believe you?" he asked gently.

"Maybe you're not a trusting soul," she said, her gaze flashing to his and back to the key.

The woman's astringent tone matched her earlier, back-off-fella attitude, and he was relieved. Her skim milk white face had disturbed him. He'd never seen himself as a man who intimidated women, and he didn't like the idea that he'd scared her. Pushing for answers was one thing, but reducing her in-your-face thorniness to white-faced fear wasn't an image of himself he cared for. "Not trusting? Me? I'm wounded," he said, placing his hand over his heart.

"Now why don't *I* believe *you?*" Her arm resting on the dog, she turned to him and lifted her eyebrow, her mockery obvious.

"How perceptive of you." Deliberately he repeated her earlier gibe and watched her quite remarkable blue eyes darken behind her glasses. "I'd almost think we'd met before—for you to have such insight into my character, Miz McDonald. Or was it only a lucky guess?" He wondered if she'd let him have the last word. He somehow didn't think she would.

"Down, Loofah," the woman said and ground the ignition key, restarting the engine before tilting her chin up at him. "Look, cowboy, you tried out your pickup routine, and it didn't work. You were bored, at loose ends, and I wasn't interested. Don't make a big deal out of it, okay? Call it a day."

Pebbles and dust spurted out from under the tires as she backed out. The monster dog watched him from the rear window, tongue hanging out as if maybe after all she'd like Buck to be dinner.

For the second time in less than twenty-four hours, Buck found himself contemplating the van's taillights. But this time, he had an answer.

She knew him. Her slightly acid responses hadn't been those of a stranger. And he knew her. But she wasn't a Miz, Ms. or Mrs. McDonald. Some other name. It would come to him sooner or later. Dust blew into his face as he stared into the empty distance.

He understood the sizzle crackling between them. He understood sex. He liked the way her pupils dilated when she looked at him. He liked the way her smooth skin shone pink with discomfort. He liked the faint scent of flowers that rose from her skin, her hair.

The sense that there was something more than a sexual pull between them disturbed him. He liked sex a whole, heaping bunch. It was simple, uncomplicated. What he felt toward the woman with the bedroom voice and cautious eyes wasn't simple at all.

Scratching the still-itching mosquito bite on his neck, he thought about the peculiar swirl of emotions the woman created in him. He'd never exerted this kind of energy in pursuit of a woman, and he wasn't comfortable with the sense that he was sailing over the edge into unknown seas, that she had some power over him.

But he trusted his instincts and his instincts told him that she had her own reasons for pretending not to remember him. He couldn't help wondering what they were. Rocking slowly back and forth on his worn-down boot heels, he stayed there until the van was nothing more than a dark speck on the red horizon.

Dust swirling and blowing around him, foretelling the coming storm, he walked around the hospital and the physical rehabilitation center for veterans. He didn't want to go back inside the hospital. Out here in the wind and dust, the air was rich with the smells of ozone and earth, with sweat and flowers. Inside the automatic doors were filtered air and the smells of disinfectant and tragedy.

Bea refused to leave. "I've slept beside Hoyt every night for almost forty years. We've never been separated. I don't intend to start now. I don't want y'all fussing me about it, hear?"

They heard. And they quit pestering her to go back to the ranch and rest. "You know how Mama is," Buck said to his brothers. "Don't push. She'll only dig in her heels harder." Like the woman in the Palmetto Mart, he thought, surprised. "I'll be here. Let's back off, all right?"

There was a curious peacefulness during the quiet night hours with the pinging bells and shushing sounds of doors opening and closing. Bea dozed beside him, her head falling to his shoulder and then snapping up as anxiety slapped her awake. Buck brought her soup and tea. Later, the tea and soup gone cold, he disposed of the paper cups.

During the night, while he sat in the pulled-up chair close to Hoyt's bed, Buck felt his stepfather's gnarled hand pull against his own.

"That you, son?" Hoyt's words were slurred and hard to hear, his effort at speech palpable.

"Yeah, Daddy, I'm here." Keeping in the shadows at the head of the bed, Buck stayed out of sight, only his touch linking him to this man he loved as much as he loved anyone in the world. He would be whoever Hoyt needed him to be, Hank or T.J. He could give Hoyt that comfort. "I won't leave," Buck said, his throat closing as he swallowed.

"Bea?" The rough hand rubbed against Buck's.

"Mama's here, too. All of us."

There was a long pause. Green spikes marched in regular waves across the heart monitor.

"Buck?"

"Yeah, Daddy?" Buck leaned forward. Even without seeing him, Hoyt knew who he was, knew he wasn't T.J. or Hank.

"Don't let Bea wear herself out, hear? You know how she gets." Hoyt's words echoed his earlier ones.

"I know how Mama gets." Buck smiled in spite of the lump in his throat. "I'll watch out for her. We'll take care of her."

"Shoot, son, sounds like y'all got me with one foot in the grave already." Hoyt's breath rattled as his chest rose laboriously up and down. "Don't go picking out my tombstone just yet." Slow, spaced out, the words fell into the quiet, the man's spirit rising above the limitations of body and tubes. "I ain't ready to call it a day, you know. I got things to do. Grandkids I ain't seen yet."

Tightening his hold around his daddy's large hand, Buck

said, "Reckon that means you want us to cancel the flowers, huh?"

The rasping cough was Hoyt's version of a chuckle. "Hell, yeah. No sense in wasting all that money. I got a few miles left. Ain't time to count me out, son."

"I won't."

Hoyt's eyes closed. "Good."

"They were awful nice flowers, Daddy."

"Hope to Billy hell they were." An almost-smile twitched the corners of Hoyt's mouth. "Y'all better show this old coot proper respect." He grunted and then was silent, his chest moving slowly, slowly, rising and falling to the regular rhythm of his sleep.

Holding Hoyt's hand between both of his, Buck stroked the rough, weathered skin as he whispered, "Hang in there, Daddy." Carefully he squeezed his father's hand. "I love you," he whispered, his throat raspy with unshed tears.

For the rest of the night as Bea and Buck alternated visits, Hoyt drifted back and forth between consciousness and wherever he'd been. Like wings beating lightly against his face, Buck felt hope settle softly in him, easing the dreadful weight of fear. What would be, would be. They would handle it. Together.

In the twilight between sleeping and waking, Buck saw a tiny red race car barreling past him over and over again while two women—one with sleek blond hair, the other with wildly tumbling curls—strolled toward him and continued past, their mocking laughs blending into one as they left him behind, alone.

And when night sounds changed to morning bustle, he sat up with a start, everything coming together in his brain with an almost audible click.

He knew damned good and well who she was.

And he was going to find her, one way or the other.

Oh, yes, he remembered Jessica Bell.

Chapter Three

"I dub thee Sir Mommy." The metal toy sword tapped Jessie's left shoulder, then her right.

Her son's excited eyes met hers as she opened them blearily. "I'm a knight of the realm, am I, love bug?"

"Yep." He stood up, wrapping the rag-tattered afghan around him. A plastic, economy-size peanut butter bucket wobbled on his head. The strap under his chin kept it from falling off. "Me and Skeezes is kings." He pointed. The dog's shaggy eyebrows supported a paper plate cut into points. Red and blue and black scribbles decorated the plate. Sparkles drifted onto the floor, onto Skeezix's coat.

Jessie yawned. "Nice hat. Skeezix, you're the next *GQ* cover."

"Skeezes is wearing the crown." Gopher frowned. "See?" He lifted the unevenly cut cardboard. "Rubies and jewels. Oxen—" he frowned again "—and turkey-something."

"Onyx and turquoise?"

Releasing his chubby grip on Skeezix's crown, Gopher nodded, sparkles floated and Skeezix sneezed.

"How silly of me. I should have known. You're a warrior king?" She tapped the top of the bucket. Snagging the strap under his chin, she tugged him toward her. "Well, this knight of the realm expects a big old smackeroo kiss from the warrior king, so pucker up, warrior king."

Gopher's soft lips puckered up, and he planted a warm, wet, sweet kiss on Jessie's mouth. The bucket smacked her in the forehead, Skeezix planted his version of a smackeroo, and the doorbell rang.

Collapsing on top of her, giggling and woofing, child and dog wrestled her off the sofa. "Wow. Now that's what I call a kiss, sugar. Haul Skeezix off me, will you?" Jessie fumbled for her glasses that had twisted off and lay buried somewhere under dog and child and cushions. "Hey, guys, anybody see my glasses?"

The doorbell rang again, two short, commanding peals.

Gopher held up her glasses. "Ransom, ransom!" Shrieking toward the door with the dog following him, he galloped around unpacked boxes and stacks of paint cans. "Ransom!"

"Never, says I, me buckeroo!" Chasing after him, Jessie leaped over a roll of wallpaper that appeared out of nowhere, staggered, and bounced off Skeezix's flank. Sliding to a halt, she extended her arms in an effort to block Gopher's feints and dodges.

"Runrunasfastas you can—" he paused for breath "—can't catch me! I'm the gingerbread man!" He lowered his head and barreled toward her.

Four and a half was a delightful age, old enough so that she could see the person her son would be, young enough for goofy kisses and games. But four and a half was hard on a thirty-five-year-old body, she thought ruefully as he slipped through her grasp like beads of mercury.

On a prolonged note, the doorbell shrilled. "Hold your horses. We're on our way," Jessie grumbled, lunging for her speed-demon child. Grabbing Gopher around the waist, she threw him over her shoulder and pulled open the door as the bell sounded again. "Good grief," Jessie muttered. "Keep your pants on, buster."

"Yep, good grief," Gopher repeated. "Keep your—"

"Enough, sugar." Jessie blew a strand of hair out of her face.

Fanny wiggling in the air and nose pointed toward the door, Gopher lifted his head. "Hey, mister. You got your pants on. Why din't you hold your horses?"

"Sorry." Jessie laughed as she scooped her hair behind her ear. Late-afternoon sun shone into her eyes, made the man in front of her a lean shadow. Peering up and clasping her son's bottom with one hand, Jessie inhaled. She didn't need her glasses to recognize trouble when it came knocking at her door. "Hello, Jonas Riley."

"And a very pleasant afternoon to you, Ms. Jessica Bell."

"My mommy's not a bell," Gopher informed him. "She's a McDonald, like old McDonald and me. Only we don't got any chickens and cows, but we got dogs, Loofah and Mitzi and this is Skeezes—" he pointed "—and I like your hat and—"

"That's enough, sugar," Jessie repeated, letting her talkative terror slide to the ground. "Hand over my glasses, please."

"Nope." Gopher stared up at her, his bare toes curled under. "Ransom first."

"George. Glasses. Now." Jessie stared him down until he reluctantly handed her her eyeglasses.

"Unfair to Gopher!" he cried, the soft mouth that had been so generous with a smackeroo now turning upside down with temper and a finely tuned sense of injustice. Snatching the afghan off the floor and wrapping himself in it, Gopher stomped away in high dudgeon, Skeezix torn between following him and staying at the door. "*Very* unfair. I captured booty. I earned a ransom," he shouted as he stormed through the swinging door to the kitchen, Skeezix trotting behind him, tail wagging like an automatic dust cloth. "And *I* am the king!"

"Tough," Jessie called after him. "But that's life outside the castle. Sometimes even the king has to yield to a higher power."

"Unfair!" The door swung shut on his words.

"Live with it, sugar." She inhaled deeply, gathering her nerve, and faced the man she'd never expected to see again, much less twice in less than forty-eight hours.

"Well, golly gee, Miz Kitty, you sure run a tight ship. No ransom? Just off to the dungeons for the mutinous troops? I reckon I'm shaking in my boots."

Jessie looked down at his boots. "They could use a shine. And they don't look as if they're moving, much less shaking."

"Appearances can be deceiving, Jessica." Five years vanished like smoke as that smooth, silky voice skimmed over her, tweaking her nerve endings, moving through her until her knees went weak.

"Apparently so." Poking the ends of her glasses through her hair and over her ears, Jessie surveyed him. "Because you sure look like a derelict without a nickel to his name, not the hottest lawyer in the South and a man with more money than's good for him. Although—" she scrutinized him with a slow up-and-down glance "—I have to admit there's something about the cowboy getup that suits you." Meeting his gaze, she gestured with her chin toward the jeans and shirt he'd worn each time she'd seen him. "Grown attached to that outfit, have you, Jonas?"

He slapped his hat against his leg. "Turned into a snob, have you, Jessica?" Back and forth, the hat whisked a slow, regular rhythm against his thigh, his muscle bunching and flexing under soft denim as he shifted his weight. "Going to invite me in?"

No question about it, Jonas was trouble.

With one arm blocking the entrance, Jessie tipped her head up and shaded her eyes. She'd be double-damned if she'd invite him in. "I'll have to admit it's nice to see you again, Jonas, but I'm terribly sorry I didn't recognize you last night—" She nodded in assumed bafflement. "If I had, we could have had a fabulous—"

"Fabulous?" A streak of amusement flashed in his eyes as he interrupted her. And in that moment she knew as if he'd spoken out loud that he hadn't forgotten *anything*.

"—time catching up on our lives, but you've caught me at a really awkward moment. Gopher and I were just leaving—"

"Was not." Gopher wound an arm around her leg and looked up at the man standing in the doorway. The plastic bucket tipped to the back of her son's head. "You're letting all the cold air out, mister. Mommy doesn't like me to hold the door open."

"Makes sense." Jonas studied her son's round face. "Gopher, is it?"

"George Robert McDonald," Gopher said and stuck out his hand. "You kin shake my hand."

Jonas did.

"Want some lemonade, mister? I made it. Sort of. I squozed a lemon. It's good lemonade." He leaned forward confidingly. "But kinda sour."

Jessie sighed. Coffee and Gopher would do her in every time. "As George so politely noticed, you're letting all the cold air out, Jonas. You might as well come in."

"Reckon I can't refuse such a graciously extended invitation now, can I?"

"You could," she muttered. "I wouldn't mind."

"Pardon?" A quizzical expression clouded his face. The picture of innocent confusion, he didn't fool her. "What did you say?"

"Nothing important." Jessie motioned him into the living room and stooped down to Gopher's level. His body language shouted his fascination with the dusty cowboy. "Sugar, why don't you take Skeezix out into the backyard?"

"Don't want to." He smiled beguilingly. "Want to visit."

"Not now, Gopher. Keep Skeezix company while he has a nice run in the yard. He needs some exercise." Reaching into her dress pocket, she pulled out a doggy treat and tucked it into her son's grubby hand. "Give Skeez a snack. Take the grapes in the fridge for yourself."

From the corner of her eye she saw Jonas's boots move out of sight. The air stirred in back of her with his movement, and the hairs on the back of her neck rose in the sudden chill. She could hear him move toward the windows, around boxes. The brown paper on a roll of wallpaper crackled as he nudged it. He was a man who could enter a room and make it his own. Whether or not the effect was intentional, she couldn't decide, but she'd seen him work his magic in a courtroom, and now, in her living room, all the energy and light centered on him. Standing up, she turned so that she could keep him and Gopher both in sight.

Watching Jonas peruse the stacks of boxes, run his thin, clever fingers over a pile of her books and settle in a dining chair he flipped around, Jessie sighed. The man claimed territory effortlessly. Give Jonas Riley a proverbial inch and he'd take the mile. Well, she'd let him past the front door, so she had no one to blame but herself. This was *her* space, not his. *She* got to set the ground rules.

And she definitely did not want to rehash old times.

"Making yourself comfortable, Jonas?" she asked politely.

His folded arms rested on the curved back of the chair. "Thank you, yes," he replied, equally polite, nodding to her.

Holding the dog treat in one hand, Gopher hopped on one foot toward Jonas. "So, mister, you got horses and cows like old McDonald?"

"Yeah, a few." Steady on Gopher, Jonas's gaze was serious. "You like horses? Cows?"

"Yeah." Gopher hopped another step.

Even the damned dog couldn't leave Jonas alone, Jessie noted grouchily. Skeezix sniffed Jonas's knee and then rested his head against his thigh, regarding him soulfully.

Jessie wanted to pull her hair. "Gopher, say goodbye to Mr. Riley. He'll be leaving shortly."

Two pairs of blue eyes met her own.

"Will I?" Jonas smiled, and her toes tingled, curled. His gaze dropped to those ten traitors.

"Oh, yes," she said, shooting him a level glance she regretted as soon as she had. "Maybe you have time for reunions, but I don't. Come on, Gopher." She took her son's hand firmly in hers, and led him to the kitchen door. "Scoot, sugar. But stay inside the fence." Shutting the door behind him, she went to the refrigerator and took out the pitcher of lemonade.

Backing up, one palm flat against the fridge door to shut it, she collided with Jonas. His hands cupped her elbows, steadying her. Face burning, Jessie slammed the door and stepped sideways, away from the heat flashing from his body, hers, she couldn't tell and didn't care. She brushed his support away. "Good grief, you make yourself at home, don't you?"

"Sorry," he said, backing away as fast as she did. "I thought you knew I was behind you."

"How would I know that? You crept in here like a thief," she said crossly. Her hip tingled where it had brushed against his thigh.

"Crept? In these? Not likely." He held up a booted foot. The thick-heeled boot spanked loudly against the linoleum floor as he put his foot down. The floorboards creaking under his boots, he took four noncreeping steps and shot her a glance over his shoulder.

"All right. Maybe you didn't sneak up on me. But I didn't hear you. I thought you were still in the living room." Cradling the cold pitcher closely to her, a barrier, she opened the cabinet and pulled out two glasses, banging them on the table. Even in the air-conditioned house, steam rose from the cloudy ice cubes she dropped into the glasses. Lemonade hissed over the cubes as she poured. She pulled out a chair. "Sit."

"That work with Skeezix?" Jonas sat, stretching out his long legs to the side. Rattling ice in the glass, he saluted her with it. "So, Jessica Bell, why did you pretend you didn't know me?"

"Why do you think I recognized you?" Taking her time, she sat down.

"Didn't you?" Sharp, determined, his eyes fastened on hers.

"Wouldn't I have said so if I did?"

"Don't know. Would you have?"

"Of course. Anything else would be—*weird*." She smiled brightly.

"And you're the last person I'd ever call weird. However—" He touched her nose and she snapped her head back.

"What on earth are you doing?" She rubbed her nose fretfully.

"Checking to see if that elegant nose is growing."

"For goodness' sake, why on earth would I pretend not to know you?" She sipped delicately from the glass and hoped he'd buy the act. "And why would I lie about something like that?" She leaned forward, curious in her own right. "At any rate, Jonas, why were you at the hospital? I hope it's nothing serious?" That much was true. She placed her glass carefully on the table. "Is everything all right?"

"Don't want to answer my questions, so you'll ask your own? I remember you used to do that." He rolled the chilled glass across his cheek. "We'll play it your way, then, Jessica. As you said earlier, nice seeing you again. How are you?" His gaze held hers as he pressed the glass against his forehead, and once more she saw the hint of exhaustion in the lines around his mouth and eyes.

Compassion moved her to say, "Better than you, apparently, Jonas, to judge by the looks of you. What happened? Did all of your investments fall out the bottom of the market?"

Setting the glass down and not answering, he looked at the table and stood up. Striding to the window, he nudged aside the curtain and watched Gopher chasing Skeezix. "Nice kid. Full of beans."

"He has his moments." Remembering some of them, Jessie smiled.

Glancing over his shoulder, Buck caught that smile, the way her face softened, and his breath hitched in his chest. "I thought you were dead set on never getting married or having a family, Jessie. You said you didn't have time for a family. All you wanted was to make partner in the firm, be the next lawyer to have her name in gold leaf on the door. But you got married after all, huh?"

Her small laugh was wryly mocking. "Things change, don't they?" Her eyes met his candidly, too frankly.

Buck felt his interest quicken. It was a myth that liars always had shifty eyes. The best ones could look you right in the eyes and lie through their teeth. And sweet, lying Jessica Bell was hiding something. "You once said marriage was a trap."

"Did I?" Cool, sophisticated, the voice reminded him of the woman he'd known, the imperturbable blonde who'd worked impossible hours, wearing herself to skin and bones and loving every minute of it.

"I never thought you'd change your mind, though. You loved being a lawyer."

"Yes. I did." Her gaze slid away from his and a wisp of hair drifted into her eyes as she shook her head. "I discovered there were things I loved more."

As she spoke, her ringless left hand tightened on the glass. He motioned to her bare finger. "Sorry. That it didn't work out."

She lifted the bowl of ice cubes, set it down, picked it up again and rose. Putting the bowl down on the counter near the sink, she sighed. "Look, Jonas, I'm not divorced. McDonald's my middle name. I use it now."

Outside, Skeezix ran between her son's legs, tipping the child on his fanny. Flinging his arms wide, George lay giggling on the ground while Skeezix licked his face. Through the muzziness in his brain, Buck sorted through her possible meanings and felt like the world's biggest fool. "Ah, I see. No ring, I assumed—"

Abruptly she dumped the ice cubes into the sink. "I'm not married."

Buck narrowed his eyes. For the first time in a long while, he found himself speechless. He didn't know what to say to her, couldn't grasp at first what she was really telling him. He glanced back at George, then at her.

"This isn't any of your business." Her tone was distant. "But since you're obviously not going to stop questioning me, you might as well know. I never got married."

"George's father?"

"Isn't important. He's not in the picture. George is mine." Passion flared in her cool voice. "*Mine.*" She clicked two ice cubes together, pushed them down the disposal, then reached for more, compulsively, he thought, as she glared at the sink.

He was genuinely embarrassed in the face of her emotion. And he found himself despising the man who'd walked out of that child's life. Heated by her anger, her fragrance rose around him, throwing him off balance and confusing him with emotions of his own as anger bubbled inside him. "I'm sorry. I didn't mean to probe—"

"Of course you did!" She flung the last cube down the disposal. "It's your nature. Interrogating people is as natural to you as breathing." Whirling to face the sink, she stared outside. "It's a game with you. You love it!"

He didn't like the picture of himself she painted. "Yeah, I like knowing why people act the way they do, so I ask questions, but I never saw myself as the kind of person who sticks pins in butterflies."

"It's not that kind of cruelty." She cast him a quick look, then glanced down, her brown eyelashes thick brush strokes against the curve of her creamy skin. "You're like a pig on the scent of truffles, that's all."

For the first time in weeks, he laughed. He couldn't help it. She'd touched his sense of the ridiculous. "A pig rooting for fungi? Root, little pig, or die?"

Her chuckle was halfhearted. "All right, I went a little overboard. At least nobody ever accused you of being a male chauvinist pig. Just relentlessly curious. It's your virtue. And your flaw."

Cutting too close to the bone, her words stung him. "Count me in the column of one more flawed human, then, and score one for you, Ms. Bell."

"I don't try to score points anymore, Jonas. I'm not Jessica Bell. I don't know who or what you came here expecting to find, but the woman you knew doesn't exist. I'm Jessie McDonald, mom, therapist." Hands bracing her on the sink, she leaned against it, head lowered, shoulders curved forward in a curiously vulnerable posture that pierced him to the heart.

"You know, all my friends and family have always called

me Buck. You're the only person who's ever called me Jonas.''

''I'm not family—''

''And we're not quite friends, are we?'' He touched her shoulder and she curled it forward even more, rejecting him. Her laugh was shaky. ''No, *friends* isn't the word, Jonas. Not for what we were.''

''Lovers?'' he asked quietly, lifting a strand of her hair and watching the light play with the colors. ''Is that what we were?''

''Oh, no, that least of all.'' She clasped her arms around her waist and moved away from him, the coil of hair trailing across his thumb like the touch of a living creature. ''Certainly not—lovers.''

''What were we, Jessica?'' He followed her as she moved restlessly from one end of the kitchen to the other.

''I'm not sure there's a word that covers that night.'' Her laugh rose, spiraled tight between them.

''But you haven't forgotten it.'' Taking her shoulders, he turned her to face him. He couldn't have explained why, but he needed to see her face when she answered him.

Meeting his, her eyes were wide, limpidly blue and candid. Beautiful, lying eyes. ''Actually, Jonas, until you rang my doorbell, I had forgotten. And if I seem a bit—uncomfortable, you can certainly understand, can't you? I mean, having you show up at my doorstep after all these years of not even thinking about you? Of course I'd forgotten that night. I had no reason to remember.''

''You can't lie worth a damn, Jessica. No wonder you decided to quit being a lawyer.''

''Or perhaps that's your ego speaking? Perhaps you can't accept the truth when you hear it?''

''Is it the truth?'' He watched her pupils darken, saw himself reflected there, and knew she'd lie again.

''Of course it is. One night, years ago. I'm sorry if your feelings are hurt, but a lot has happened since. I've been busy. New career. New life.'' She turned her head to watch her child turning cartwheels end over end down the length of the yard.

Watching him with her, Buck was struck by a sense of familiarity, by a sense of loss. Maybe it was nothing more than having been at T.J.'s ranch with all the Tyler kids running around and realizing the emptiness of his goals, the dead end his life had become.

Her question brought him back to her.

"Are you still with Collins, Keane and Riley?" Walking to the kitchen table with a dishrag, she skirted him with what he concluded was her version of subtlety. Elbows close to her rib cage, chin a tad too elevated, her body language gave away her awareness of him.

"No."

"I'm surprised. You loved being in the courtroom. The energy, the battle. You versus everybody else."

"Yes. I loved it." He remembered. And he still missed the adrenaline rush.

"Funny, isn't it, that we both left? Neither of us could see anything else except the goal of winning. Career-driven, we were two of a kind with no room in our lives for anything else. Nothing else was as important to either of us, was it?" Not looking at him, she touched a wet spot on the shiny table and rubbed the moisture dry. "Except you'd already made your reputation. You gave up more than I did." She draped the rag over the faucet. The thin strap of her dress slid down her arm, drew his eyes to the curve of her breasts as she leaned against the sink. "You had the world on a string. You had everything you wanted."

"I thought I did." His mouth went dry as he watched the pull of fabric lift and tighten, shape the sweet roundness of breasts and hips.

"What changed your mind?"

"I won a case I should have lost." He stirred, hooked his thumbs in his belt loops, inhaled. "I decided that I didn't want to be a lawyer after all." He wondered if she'd ask which case.

She didn't. Her hands on the sink went utterly still. Then, taking a deep breath that lifted her breasts, she spoke. "And now you're a—cowboy?"

"A rancher."

"Do you like ranching?"

"I reckon. Anyway, it's what I do now."

"Is it enough?"

Buck thought for a moment. He'd been filled with such self-disgust, such revulsion, that he'd run as far away and as fast as he could from what he'd spent his life achieving. "I thought it would be. It was different from the law. I wanted something clean, simple."

"But you're not a simple man, Jonas."

"Apparently not. I'd hoped I was." In the past few weeks he was learning more about himself than he wanted to know.

She smoothed the rag flat and then turned around. "And do you have children? A wife?" Her voice was only mildly interested, but her grip on the rag betrayed her.

"No."

"I guess I'm not surprised. Everybody knew you weren't marriage material. You were Jonas Buckminster Riley, the *very* eligible bachelor." The sideways tilt of her head was teasing. Her eyelashes lifted, lowered, as she added in a wry tone, "No wonder you have ego problems."

"Ego?" He frowned. "Not me."

"Hmm. Yes, Jonas, I'm sorry to disillusion you, but in fact your ego is quite strong. You're a very secure man. I think you don't expect rejection, failure." Her mouth lifted in a generous sweep of pink that couldn't quite hide the barb. "It's probably an unconscious assumption on your part. You expect everything to go the way you want it to. Usually it does. If you'd wanted a family, Jonas, you'd have the requisite trophy wife and two and a half kids by now."

Her comment rubbed that raw place in his soul. He shrugged. "So maybe you're right. Maybe I wasn't looking to settle down. Anyway, I wasn't a good candidate for marriage."

"And now?"

His gaze drifted to Gopher and Skeezix outside. "I don't know. I've never seen myself married. But I don't know what I want anymore. Reckon I've fallen into a midlife crisis? Or maybe I'm hearing the ticking of my biological clock?'' He meant the comment to be lighthearted, but it held a truth he understood only after he spoke, and he wished he could call back the words hanging too heavily between them.

"Could be." She lifted her hand as though to touch him, then let it fall to her side. But her voice was unexpectedly gentle. "Does all this self-analysis have anything to do with why you were at the hospital?"

"Very good. I'm impressed." He clapped his hands together, stalling. "You haven't lost all your technique, Jessica. Still can't be diverted from a question you want answered, can you?"

"I'm sorry, Jonas. I was prying." She turned her head sideways to check outside and then returned her gaze to him, her eyes soft with regret. "I didn't mean to cause you pain. I was concerned, that's all. You look so tired." She smiled, such an understanding, giving smile that Buck wanted to walk over to her and fold her in his arms, to fill himself with her warmth.

The afternoon sun glowed against the scuffed planks of her kitchen, touched her cheek with rosy gold as she watched her son. The moment was unexpectedly peaceful, healing, loosening the cold knot deep inside him, the lump that had settled there during the long hours at the hospital.

Before he realized what he was doing, he found himself telling her about Hoyt.

When he finished, she said, "I remember your dad. He came to the office once when I was there. On your birthday, I think. I liked him."

"Yeah. He took me to lunch. Said it wasn't every day a man's—" Buck swallowed "—oldest son turned thirty."

Maybe it was the way Jessie's face softened, her mouth loosening in sympathy, her body bending unconsciously toward him; maybe it was all the loneliness balled up inside him looking for a way out; or maybe after all it *was* simple, a man wanting a woman. But whatever the reason, he reached out and brushed his thumb across the pink fullness of her lips. "You have the prettiest mouth, Jessie. Did you know that?" He traced the smooth arc of her bottom lip. "I've always loved your mouth. Soft, like nothing I've ever touched." He took a step, closing the space between them.

As he stroked the corners of her lips, fascinated by the tiny indentations, their satin-smoothness, her mouth parted. She didn't move, and he took that final step, his right boot sliding between her bare feet, and discovered that nothing at all was simple about what he felt when he touched her.

More than a man wanting a woman, much more, this deep humming inside him that turned the room airless and hot, drew him to her, made him crave the touch of Jessie's skin against his. No, definitely not *a* woman's touch. *Jessie's.*

Sliding his fingers through the wild curls that had tempted him even before he realized who she was, he cupped her head with his palms, his thumbs pressing lightly, lightly against the corners of her mouth. "May I kiss you, Jessie McDonald? For old times' sake? For my sake?"

He thought she moved, nodded. Maybe she did. He lowered his mouth to hers. Warm, all that softness yielding to the insistence of his lips and tongue, her lips met his, and her body seemed to curl against him.

Or maybe not.

All he knew in that moment as he pulled her to him was that her touch soothed the ache inside him, made him feel as though the world was still a good place to be, made him forget the darkness moving through him.

And as he kissed her, finding refuge in the touch of her, he glimpsed in the strip of window over her shoulder the boy wrestling with the monster dog, both rolling over and over on the ground in the fading glow of sunshine.

"Jonas," she whispered, and her small hands stole around his neck, tracing the edge of his shirt. "This isn't a good idea."

"No," he muttered, lifting her against him, her toes settling on his boots, "probably not."

She was the same. She was different. The woman he'd taken into his bed, the woman who'd welcomed him into herself so long ago had been all nerves and lovely angles, edgy, like a racehorse. *This* woman, *Jessie,* was curved, soft, her skin as warm as a sun-ripened peach. But the generosity of response, ah, that was the same, the same, he thought, as she opened her mouth and he tasted her. Slanting his mouth over hers, he groaned and lifted her higher, needing something from her that he couldn't begin to name, knowing only that in the taste and scent of this woman he could ease the loneliness, the coldness; in her he could forget the despair riding him.

Only in her could he escape himself.

"Jessie, please," he whispered, and didn't know what he was asking for. "Touch me," he said finally, taking her hand and placing it under his shirt, next to his skin. Her fingers flexed against him, a small, scrabbling movement that sparkled through him, turning the darkness behind his eyelids to rich red. His blood pounded thick and heavy, a sweetness that hurt.

She slid her arm around his waist, and her tiny cry as she traced the length of his spine arrowed through him.

"Jessie, Jessie," he whispered, bending his knees and tracing the beat of her pulse down her throat, over the curve of her breast, nudging aside thin cotton to find creamy skin.

"Jonas." And his name became a sigh, a plea in her husky voice. "Jonas." Her mouth moved against his chin, and she sank into him, her leg moving restlessly against his, her right knee rising, falling, until he anchored it against his thigh, his hand curved around the swell of calf muscle, stroking.

"Get away from my mommy, mister!" Something slapped against the back of Buck's knees, then slapped again. "I mean it!"

One hand still holding Jessie's palm flat against his chest, Buck looked up, down, and finally into the angry face of Jessie's child.

"Gopher," she murmured. Her mouth was red, swollen. Freeing her hand from Buck's shirt, she caressed Gopher's head. "Sugar, he's not hurting me."

As her son whacked him steadily against the calves and knees, Buck lifted her off his boots and stepped back.

"I don't like you, mister!"

Staring bleakly at Jessie's small defender, Buck admitted the unpleasant truth to himself. Like that night years ago, he'd

Chapter Four

Low in the west, purple-tinged pink streaked the sky, yielding to darkness even as Buck spoke.

"Jessie, I'm sorry. I wasn't thinking." Standing beside the open door of his Jeep, one foot resting inside, he was at a loss for words. Seeing himself through the kid's eyes had wrenched him from his self-absorbed plunge into the sweetness of Jessie's touch, a moment in which he'd thought of nothing except his own need, his own hunger.

The protective anger in Jessie's son's eyes had been humiliating.

"It's okay, Jonas." Evening shadowed Jessie's face, made it mysterious to him, and even with the memory of his selfishness lingering, he longed to trace those shadowy contours of Jessie McDonald.

"I wasn't thinking about George, about his coming in. I feel lousy that he—"

"Jonas." Jessie's hand fluttered in the air, a small, sturdy bird winging against night, falling as she continued, "Gopher didn't understand, that's all. What happened wasn't your fault."

"Hell it wasn't." Buck flipped the door lock up and down.

"I wasn't thinking. I showed up at your doorstep, practically forced my way in—"

"Yes, I noticed how you stuck your foot between the door and the doorjamb, giving me no option whatsoever except to invite you in, slavering beast that you are." Even in the dark he could see the gleam of her eyes as she rolled them.

That tender flutter of her hand had affected him in some indefinable way, its vulnerability painful as it fell to her side, and now her gritty independence moved him, deepened his feelings of guilt and forced him to acknowledge what he'd seen in her eyes when she opened her door. "You didn't want me to come in."

Her mouth tightened. "No, Jonas, I didn't."

"So there you are." He whacked the door of the Jeep with his fist. "Your son's upset and it's my fault."

She looked heavenward. The glow of her porch light gilded the line of her slim throat, a curve of gold in the darkness. "Lord deliver me from patronizing men."

"I'm not patronizing you, Jessie." Resting his chin on top of the Jeep door, he sighed. "But that look on your boy's face sure put me in my place. I shouldn't have put the moves on you."

"Put the moves on me?" Gripping the door with both hands, she shook it, dislodging his chin. "You arrogant, pig-headed—" She stopped, took a deep breath, her cheeks puffing, and blew it out, her breath falling gently on him with sweet-scented warmth. "Okay. Let me get this clear in my poor, muddled feminine brain, all right?" Counting off on her fingers, she said, "One, you're a skunk, a scoundrel, a rat. And two, I'm a swooning, helpless Victorian spinster who doesn't have the sense God gave a flea? This explanation makes you feel better?"

"When you put it that way—"

Full speed ahead, she ran right over his words. "Well, buster, listen to what you're implying, will you, please? Even if that kind of apology lets you off the hook, do you think that world view makes *me* feel better? That I'm some passive feminine object? With no mind or will of my own?"

"No, of course not, but you're twisting what I meant. Come on, Jessie, we both know you didn't want to have anything to do with me, but I kept pushing. First at the Palmetto Mart, and then here tonight. I took advantage of you."

"Took advantage of me?" Her hand closed tighter on the door and, nodding, he moved out of range.

"That's how I see it," he said grimly, knowing it was the truth. He'd used the analgesic of sex and hormones to avoid thinking. And it had worked, at least until Gopher attacked his ankles. Buck really couldn't give himself a pass—not knowing what he understood about his motivations, he sure couldn't—so he insisted stubbornly, "I took advantage of the situation."

"What century were you born in, Jonas?" she asked in an acidly sweet voice. "In case you haven't noticed, I'm perfectly capable of taking care of myself, which, for your information, includes avoiding unwanted males. You think I can't take care of myself? Believe me, Jonas, I can. I have. And I'm not anybody's pushover."

"I never said you were."

"You implied I was. Same difference."

"Jessie, I'm bigger, stronger."

"So you are. But I don't like thinking of myself as a— victim, so I've learned how to take care of myself, okay?" She gave the door another yank.

"Guys have that advantage I mentioned, and it sure seems to me that I used mine." He steadied the car door against her push.

"Jonas, listen carefully. No matter what you think, no matter what you intended, you didn't push." She kicked a rock with her foot. "Aggravated the heck out of me, yes. But it was only a kiss between—old acquaintances, let's say. Nothing more. No big deal. Let's forget it, okay?" She squared her shoulders and looked him straight in the eyes.

"No big deal, huh?"

"Not even a little deal." Her smile flashed in the darkness.

Buck couldn't forget the boy's fierceness. "What about Gopher? It was a big deal to him."

"I'll explain. He'll be fine. He misunderstood, that's all."

She seemed too casual about her son's reaction, not at all disturbed by it, and Buck seized on the idea that sprang full-blown into his mind with her comment. Once the thought crossed his mind, he found he wanted confirmation. "This is the first time he's seen you kissing someone, being kissed?" He didn't want to think about why he needed to know. "Doesn't he see you with men? When you date?"

"When I date?" The breeze trailed a curl across her cheek and she tucked it firmly in back of her ear. "Okay, Jonas, let's clarify the issue here."

He'd seen her use that same logical approach to case discussions during meetings. Jessica had always wanted everything out on the table, unambiguous.

Digging her feet into the pebbles and grass of the driveway, she proceeded to spell it out for him, irritation pulling her eyebrows into a thin, silky brown line. "What are you asking? Do you want to know if I see other men occasionally? Frequently? A *lot* of other men? If I'm involved with a—what's the term?—significant other? Well," she said, tapping his chest, "like Gopher's father, this is none of your business, either. Think what you want to, Jonas. I couldn't care less. Now, what was your point?"

"Reckon I didn't have one. You proved your case, Jessica." He swung himself into the Jeep. He figured he couldn't begin to make her understand, and maybe his sense of guilt over the incident didn't matter to anybody but himself. But guilt unresolved left responsibility lying heavily on him.

"Fine. Then we can forget this." She crossed her arms under her breasts. They lifted, a soft roundness under night-dark fabric, a reminder that she had changed. Jessica or Jessie, something in her pulled at him.

"Gopher's a swell kid, Jessie." Seeing the small shadow that had sidled out from behind the bush next to the driveway, Buck added, "And brave. What he did took real courage."

The shadow pressed into the folds of Jessie's skirt. She put her arm around his shoulder and drew him closer. "Hey, sugar. I thought I told you to stay inside?"

"Did." Gopher wrapped himself in a swath of skirt fabric and scrutinized Buck. "You wasn't hurting my mommy?"

"No." Buck stepped back out of the Jeep and hunkered a few feet away from Jessie's pint-size guardian. "But it looked like I was, huh?"

"Maybe." Scowling at him, Gopher didn't look convinced.

"I wasn't, Gopher. I would never hurt your mother."

"What was you doing?"

Buck looked helplessly up at Jessie, who merely lifted her eyebrow. Buck shifted, his boots kicking up spurts of dust. "I kissed her. She kissed me."

"Huh." Deep skepticism flickered over Gopher's face as he announced, "Mommy kisses me. That wasn't kissing."

"Want to help me out here, Jessie?"

"Nope." Her expression was angelic. All that was missing was the halo. "You're doing really swell on your own, cowboy." The indentations at the corners of her mouth swept up before she brought the swoop of lower lip under control. "Go right ahead, Jonas."

Buck gave up. In spite of nieces and nephews, he was on his own in unfamiliar territory without a compass or a guide. Well, he'd known he wasn't meant for this whole baby and kid scene. Balancing his hands on his knees, he plunged ahead. "Gopher, I wasn't hurting her. Grown-ups, men and women, well…" He paused, casting a desperate glance at Jessie, who continued to ignore him. "They kiss differently. Not the same way moms kiss kids. It's different. It's a, well, you've seen people kissing on television, right?"

Gopher wrinkled his nose. "Yep. *Very* silly."

"That's the kind of kiss your mom and I were sharing."

Gopher studied Buck while a line of flop sweat trickled down Buck's back as he waited for Gopher's response.

"A TV kiss?"

Buck nodded. Jessie snickered.

Finally Gopher scratched his nose. "You swear on lizard guts and fish bones you wasn't hurting her?"

"That's a new one," Buck muttered. He, T.J. and Hank had been creative with swears and oaths, but lizard guts? Fish bones? Oaths were sworn on valued objects. Where was the kid coming from? Had the world changed that much in thirty-four or -five years? "Made it up, did you?"

"Maybe." Gopher watched him steadily. "You solemnly swear? 'Cause if you don't, I'll have to fight you, maybe."

Seeing the grave assessment in Gopher's eyes, Buck knew the answer was important. The oath might be a child's oath, a made-up one, but the boy needed a serious response. Raising his hand, Buck said, "I solemnly swear on fish bones and lizard guts that I was not hurting your mother."

The relief that washed over the boy's face made the absurd oath worthwhile. Gopher took a step forward, dragging Jessie with him. "And I was brave?"

"Like—" Who the hell did kids this age admire? The first name that popped into his mind was one from childhood stories Hoyt had read to him. "Like Richard the Lionhearted."

"Yep. He was brave. He was a king like me." Gopher kept his gaze intently on Buck, clearly waiting for some sign or gesture that escaped Buck. "But Lionheart went somewhere with Robin Hood. I forget."

"To the Crusades," Buck said, still squatting in front of this child whose quizzical eyes struck him with a sense of recognition. Like T.J.'s Charlie, or Gracie, Jilly's little girl Hank had adopted, Gopher shared a terrifying innocence, and Buck hated to disappoint the kid by not knowing how to conclude their conversation. But search as hard as he could, damned if he wasn't clueless. Buck started to straighten up. "Your mom's lucky to have a son who's strong and brave, Gopher."

Then, looking down at the disappointed face of the boy with his outstretched sword hand, Buck got it. Men shook hands to show respect. Well, hell's bells, kings required an entirely different courtesy.

Kneeling on one knee and hoping Jessie didn't hear the creaks and pops of his almost-forty-year-old knees, Buck inclined his head. "So, your majesty, having sworn the royal oath, I ask your forgiveness."

Gopher nodded his head regally and tapped him on the shoulder. "Okay. Rise, Sir Cowboy."

Surrendering to a momentary fancy, Buck rose in his most knightlike manner. He didn't dare look at Jessie for fear he'd break out in whoops. "Thanks, King."

"Very nice, Jonas. Excuse me, *Sir* Cowboy." Jessie wondered if the darker tinge to his cheekbones was a flush of embarrassment. In the few years she'd worked with him and the other lawyers in the firm Jonas had helped start, she'd never glimpsed this whimsical side. That Jonas, the man with his quietly understated thousand-dollar suits and black Porsche had been afflicted with a terminal case of tunnel vision. This man in his beat-up jeans and dusty boots entered her son's world. She liked the cowboy Jonas better, she decided, startled into immobility as he strode closer.

"Thanks for your hospitality, Jess," he said slyly, extending one work-roughened hand, and the zinger came straight out of the old Jonas.

"You're welcome." She shook his hand, amused in spite of everything that had happened by the formality of their exchange in front of Gopher.

"Bye, Mr. Sir Cowboy," Gopher added, sticking out his grubby hand. "See you."

"Maybe sometime—"

"I don't think so—"

Jessie's words banged up against Jonas's. "Sugar, say good-night and go on inside. Mr. Riley is leaving. We'll have supper in a minute. Will you take the Jell-O out for me, please? Choose the flavor you want."

"Banas and strawbaby." Sticking his sword in a cardboard container slung with rope across his back, Gopher trudged toward the front door, thinking. "Maybe not."

"Clever. Would he have given you an argument if you hadn't distracted him?"

"A discussion, Jonas, a discussion," she said wryly. "He discusses, you see. At least that's his term for it." She traced a circle in the grass and pebbles. "Lawyering must be bred in the bones, you suppose?"

Stepping into the Jeep, Jonas hesitated. "It must have been hard, raising him on your own?"

He had no idea, and she wasn't about to tell him about the lonely nights and exhausting days and the fear nibbling at her every minute of the day, fear that she was making mistakes every time she made a decision, fear that something would happen to her and Gopher would be left without anyone, fear— Jessie reined in the thoughts he'd triggered. Oh, she knew they'd come creeping in again at three or four in the morning when loneliness and fatigue stripped away her defenses. They always did. She was beginning to suspect that every single parent was prey to those blue meanies lying in wait in the darkest hours.

"Jess?" The quiet voice brought her back. "Was it difficult? On your own?"

For now, however, she could pretend. She met his gaze squarely. "Not too bad." Perhaps it was the unspoken sympathy in his low drawl, but suddenly she longed to unburden herself, to tell him about trying to work after sleepless nights, about balancing a work schedule with a sick baby. She didn't. With long practice, she squashed the need to spill her worries onto someone else. She'd made her decision. Or it had been made for her. "I had resources. I'm luckier than most single mothers."

"Resources, huh?" His elegantly bent nose tipped down as he scrutinized her.

She was glad he was in the Jeep. Distance provided safety. "I had money, an education. Resources, Jonas."

"But no partner, no one to help?"

Damn him. "No."

"Do you regret not marrying Gopher's father?"

"Never," she said fiercely, too fiercely, because he went very still in the face of her passion. "I love my son. We're a family, the two of us. It's enough." Jessie wished he'd fire up the engine, roar out of her driveway, back wherever he'd come from. She didn't need these reminders tonight. "Not for one minute do I regret anything that's happened. Even if I could change one second of the past, I wouldn't."

"Really?" Sadness lingered in his low-pitched question. "I'd change a lot of things. If I could."

"I wouldn't." She'd worked her way down a rocky road to where she was, and she knew the cost better than anyone, but how could she even think about regretting the steps that had brought her to this point? She'd made choices without being able to see the future, but they'd been her decisions, her choices. No one else's. She could live with them.

"Hard to believe, Jess, that you wouldn't change anything. You're a lucky woman, then. To have no regrets. Most people have a lot of them. Events, moments in their life that they'd alter if given another chance. But you wouldn't."

She heard the question behind his statement, knew it referred to a night he'd obviously forgotten until she bumped into him at the Palmetto Mart, knew what he was asking her, but she couldn't answer any more directly than she already had, so, once more, she skirted the issue. "I'm sorry, Jonas, that your life hasn't worked out the way you wanted it to." She wondered for a second if the faded jeans and run-down boots represented more than hard work and a life-style changed not by choice but by financial reversal. He never had answered her roundabout question concerning his investments. "And I'm terribly sorry about your dad. Is there any way I can help?"

He clicked the key over. Such a small, quiet sound of withdrawal. "Thanks, but I don't think so."

"I'm at the hospital every day. Usually in the VA wing. I'm the recreational therapist, and I organize activities and nonphysical therapy for the vets. I use the dogs in pet therapy in the pediatric oncology unit and in surgery rehabilitation."

"Pet therapy?"

"Therapy dogs. Cats, birds, sometimes horses."

"Horses?" He shook his head.

She smiled at his look of disbelief. "That's right. Horses. But we don't take them into the hospital, if that's what you're thinking." Jessie wanted him to see how important this work, so different from what she'd once done, was. "Some recreational therapists are trained and certified by a national group to work as partners with animals in particular treatment programs. Our hospital has several Delta-certified animal/human teams. We work a lot with geriatric patients, too.''

"I can see how animals would distract patients.''

"The animals are wonderful. You can't imagine the difference they make until you've seen it. Anyway, Jonas, sometimes I'm at the VA center in the evenings if we've planned a special events speaker. I'd be happy to look in on your dad, see how he's doing. The intensive care unit is on my regular route, anyway.'' Not sure why she was volunteering, Jessie wound down. "I know the nurses over on the sixth floor. I could talk to them for you. If you want. Well, I suppose with your brothers and their wives, your mom, you don't need anyone else.''

At those words, Jonas turned. His face was somber and he looked at her for the longest time, staring until Jessie thought he must be memorizing every line in her face. "No, I don't need anyone,'' he said. His hands tightened around the steering wheel, loosened. "Thanks for the offer, but we have the whole clan there in shifts. Except for Mama. We can't get her to leave.''

"I understand.''

"Yeah.'' The engine continued to idle as Jonas sat there running his hands around and around the steering wheel. "Yeah, everybody's staying at T.J.'s ranch. All the kids. Mama and Daddy had moved back from Seattle, and we had a birthday party for her.'' The sound of the car engine seemed to reverberate through Jessie with the same kind of deep-down melancholy she heard in Jonas's voice and didn't understand. "All those kids. Mama and Daddy's grandkids.''

"And you don't have any children,'' she said gently, wondering how Jonas fit into that family-oriented setup, loner that he'd always been.

"No. I never wanted children.''

"And now you're rethinking some of your choices.''

"Shoot.'' He shot her a grin that curled her toes with its blend of mockery and sadness. "Reckon my biological clock's ring-a-dinging after all?''

"Could be," she said, catching a glimpse of a buried pain in the way he kept the grin a shade longer than natural. "Everybody's different, though. What works for your brothers might not work for you. I'm sure they had their reasons for settling down, having children."

"I like your son, Jessie."

She swallowed shakily. He'd surprised her. "Me too. I'm kind of fond of him."

"Go give the king his supper, Jess. Royalty shouldn't be kept waiting too long." With that, he engaged the gears and did a fast bootlegger turn out of the driveway and into the road.

"Damn you, Jonas," she whispered, her throat closing. "Just had to have the last word, didn't you?"

For long minutes she stayed where she was, breathing in the sultry, jasmine-scented air, remembering another night.

Inside, returning to the present, she clicked off the porch light and went into the kitchen. "Hey, love bug," she said and ruffled the sweat-stiff hair of her son. "We'll make Jell-O while the porcupine peppers are warming up, okay?"

"'Kay." Gopher handed her the cardboard box of flavored gelatin. "When's Mr. Cowboy coming back?"

"Mr. Riley, sugar."

"When."

"He won't be back, Gopher. This was a onetime visit."

"Oh." Sticking his finger into pink powder, he licked it clean, then redipped. "He *might* come again." Pink powder ringed his pursed mouth. "He might."

"Oh, Gopher, sugar-pie, please don't set your hopes on seeing him again. We ran into each other at the grocery store. He wanted to see how I was doing, that's all. Truly, Gopher, don't expect him to come back. He won't."

"Maybe." Gopher took a handful of canned fruit cocktail and dumped it into the dissolved powder. "But he might." He nodded confidently.

Jessie sighed. "He might."

The microwave bell sounded. "Porky pines!" Gopher trotted to the table and collapsed into a chair.

"Uh, sugar?"

He looked at her. Dirt smeared one cheek, pink Jell-O powder had dribbled onto his shirt, and the tips of four fingers were stained bright pink. "Yep?"

"Wash your hands."

"Don't see why. I already been eating with 'em."

"It's one of those goofy rules."

"Huh."

A couple of hours in Jonas's company, and Gopher was picking up the man's speech habits. Jessie sighed again. If she didn't watch out, she was going to turn into one of those women who sighed every other word. And she'd never been a sigher. Not until Jonas had walked into her life again, that is. Like sighing, he was a bad habit.

She'd kicked her Jonas habit once. She didn't think she could go through withdrawal again.

Cleaning up the kitchen table with Gopher's erratic help after rice-and-ground-beef-stuffed green peppers, the rice grains sticking up like porcupine quills, Jessie thought again about the dark lines of weariness under Jonas's eyes, his disreputable clothes. She liked the look of him in the tight, weathered jeans and worn straw cowboy hat. She didn't like the idea that he might be down on his luck at all, and the idea that he might be in a financial bind troubled her as she splashed Gopher with soapy bathwater, playing his version of "sink the soap" until the bathroom floor was sopping wet.

"Out."

"Nope." He lay on his back, his nose, toes and fingertips breaking the surface of the water. "Not done."

Lifting him clear of the tub, Jessie threw a dry towel on the floor to soak up the slop. "Sorry, warrior king, but even kings leave their castle when the hundred-year flood hits. Careful." She set him up on the counter in front of the mirror.

Twisting, he watched himself in the mirror. Lifting his hand, he flattened his water-darkened shampooed hair. Blue eyes met blue eyes in the mirror. "Mr. Riley has eyes like mine and yours," he announced with satisfaction as he stretched his eyelids up and pulled his eyebrows straight across his forehead.

"So he does, sugar. Now, ready for the mummy wrap?"
She swathed him in a large cartoon-character-garish beach
towel, wrapping it around and around his body and making a
head covering out of the pointed end. "There." She stood him
up on the counter and let him face the mirror. "The Mummy
King."

Gopher laughed. Extending his arms and curving his fingers
into claws, he moaned, *"A-ooo, a-ooo."* His eyes shone back
at her. *"A-ooo, ooo.* Are you scared, Mommy?"

"Terrified," she said and buried her face in his sweet-
smelling neck, inhaling the soapy-clean fragrance of her nonstop child.

When she'd finally tucked him in, read three stories to him,
and told him two more, Jessie wanted to sink into the nearest
chair and zone out. The thought of waking up to a sink filled
with dirty dishes and dried-on food kept her moving. Jonas
had asked her if it was difficult being on her own. She wondered how much harder it would become.

Because it would.

Gopher would learn to ride a bike. Drive a car. And each
new skill would take him farther away from her, take him
where she couldn't protect him.

She wouldn't think about it. Not tonight.

And she didn't.

Instead she thought about the years that had passed, the
changes in Jonas Riley. Sticking dishes into the dishwasher
and wiping up the bathroom, she sorted out the conflicting
impressions and began to see where the cowboy persona was
nothing more than an extension of his "good ol' boy" routine
from the years when she'd known him. The clever, aggressive
lawyer and the rustic, drawling cowboy were genuine, both
facets of the same man. As she'd told him, he was a complicated man.

Before midnight, she finally crawled between her sheets, the
throbbing of the air conditioner an ominous hint of a bill looming on the horizon. Tuning the radio to an all-music, all-night
station, she lay on her side, curled around her pillow. A
mournful trumpet solo rose and fell softly in the hushed room,

weaving in between the shadows and memories. Holding the pillow tight, she listened to the notes, the pickup of the rhythm section coming in, *shhh-shh, shhh-shh,* softly, softly, echoing the rhythm of her heartbeat, *shhh-shh.*

She was almost asleep when the muted warble of the phone mingled with the final trumpet notes. "Yes?"

"Did I wake you, Jess?" Low and intimate in her ear, Jonas's voice slid over the wire, into her, *shhh-shh.*

"What do you think?" She drew her knees up against the pillow and turned her head so that the pillow supported the receiver.

"You sound sleepy. That's what I think." His voice sighed into her ear, shivering the hairs along her arm with pleasure. "Bad idea, this phone call."

"Why did you call, then?" She tucked the receiver closer. "Most people are in bed by now."

"I can see you in that bed, Jessie. A small, narrow one, right?"

Jessie stretched one arm out to the far side of her solitary queen-size bed. "Why did you call, Jonas? Where are you?"

"I'm at the hospital, doing the night shift like I told you." Emptiness hummed down the wire. Then a whisper of breath that teased her nerve endings. "I don't know why I called you, Jess. And that's the God's honest truth. I knew you'd probably be asleep, but I walked out here to the phone, and next thing I knew, I'd dialed you up."

"How did you find my number, Jonas? It's unlisted."

"Yeah. I found that out when I went thumbing through the book for J. McDonald. Hell of a lot of McDonalds in this county, Jess, did you know that? But no J. McDonald on Floribunda Drive."

"Interesting, Jonas, but how did you find my number?" Jessie moved her flat palm against the skin-warmed cotton of her pillowcase, the smooth fabric slick against her fingertips.

"A friend."

"Hmm. Have one of your old buddies from the police run a check?"

"Now why would you think that?" he countered.

"Because, like me, Jonas, you have resources."

"I could have used the reverse listing directory. Found the number from the address."

"You could have," she agreed. The next musical piece began, an old Peggy Lee favorite of her parents', something about heat, steam heat. Jessie pleated the edge of the sheet lying over her. Steam heat and Jonas's drawl tickled her ear. Restlessly she flipped to her other side. "But you didn't, did you, Jonas?"

"No. It would have taken too long."

"Why did you wake me up, Jonas? It's late and I have to work tomorrow."

"I know. I'm sorry, Jess." The sound of a pencil tapping against a wall or a shelf traveled over the wire.

Jessie decided she liked the idea of phones with telephone wires. The line was a visible connection between two people, linking them in the night hours. You didn't get that kind of symbolism with a cordless phone. She thumped her pillow. "How's your dad?"

The silence across the miles lengthened while Peggy Lee crooned easily, perfectly, about heat. Jessie's feet were hot and she shucked off the sheet.

"He's better, I think. More alert. The test results haven't come back, though. He went to sleep a few minutes ago." His drawl sharpened. "We were talking. And then he drifted off."

"And you came out of his room and called me."

"Yeah." In her imagination, Jessie saw him slumped against the wall, his forehead resting on the painted plaster. "That's what I did."

"Mommy? I had a bad dream." Trailing his binkie-blanket, Gopher stood by her bed, rubbing his eyes and scowling.

"I hear the king," Jonas murmured.

"Yes." Jessie patted the bed beside her. "C'mon, sugar, climb in."

"Interesting idea," Jonas drawled. "But I reckon you're not talking to me, are you, Jess?"

That heat Peggy Lee had been talking about flushed over Jessie. "Idiot," she said. "And, yes, this time I'm talking to you.'' She drew the sheet over Gopher, who'd stuck a satin edge of his blanket into his mouth, stroking it with a bent forefinger, his eyes already shut, his chunky little body warm against her. "Jonas, go have a cup of hot tea. Take a nap." She knew why he'd called her. "Late night's a lousy time to be wandering around awake in a hospital."

"Yeah. It is."

She wrapped the phone cord around her hand, thinking, before she added, "Listen, I don't mind. That you called. I was listening to the radio. I hadn't gone to sleep yet. I lied about your waking me."

"I know. Good night, Jess." His drawl deepened, became a resonance vibrating through her. "Sleep tight."

"You, too," she whispered, but the receiver clicked even as she spoke. "You, too, Jonas." He wouldn't, and she ached for the desolation she sensed in him.

With her son snuggled against her and the sound of Jonas's drawl lingering, Jessie hung up the phone and shut her eyes, a bluesy guitar strumming low and lonely in the background, as lonely as the memory of Jonas's voice traveling down the telephone wires to her.

Chapter Five

Lugging her satchel filled with uncompleted reports and patient files, Jessie stepped off the elevator into the controlled chaos of the sixth floor.

Skirting the aide trundling a five-foot-high metal food cart, she headed toward the fort, the glassed-in area where the nurses and doctors coordinated schedules, paperwork and orders. Checking for the laminated wall chart listing patients' names and room assignments, she dodged the nurse trotting down the corridor.

"Whoops, Jessie. Sorry!" Pam sped down the hall.

"No problem," Jessie called, but the brown-haired nurse had already disappeared into a room where a white placard on the door instructed anyone entering to wear a mask and wash hands.

The rule on the sixth was, lead, follow, or get out of the way. Nobody on the sixth dawdled.

Underpaid, overworked and understaffed, the inmates of the sixth each did the work of four people. As hard as Jessie worked, the people on the sixth stepped it up two notches higher, keeping track of calls, dosages and patient idiosyncrasies. Not perfect, not superhuman, they did a superhuman job with grace and compassion. She was in awe of them. She loved them.

And sometimes she wondered if they had a life outside the hospital. She didn't see how they could have an ounce of energy left once they left the confines of the sixth floor. The human body and psyche, even for the people who worked the sixth, had their limitations.

Jessie checked the room assignments. Hoyt Tyler was in the last room down the hall. Reconsidering, she hesitated. She hadn't really thought this visit through. She'd definitely be intruding on Jonas and his family. Did she want to do that? More important, *could* she do it? She wasn't good with families in crisis. One-on-one, she could handle, but she'd never understood family dynamics with their swampy mix of emotion and history. Families had their own language, their own private codes, and she'd never learned the lingo. She picked at the nylon cover of her satchel, wrinkling her nose, as her annoyance grew.

Regardless of her reasons, popping into Hoyt Tyler's room unannounced, uninvited, would be awkward. Lord knew she avoided awkwardness whenever possible. She'd be in the way. Uncomfortable. Scraping her fingernail slowly across the nylon, she listed the reasons for about-facing and trekking to the elevator. "I'd make a fool out of myself," she muttered. Nobody liked to look ridiculous. Why should she put herself through an ordeal? "Absurd," she mumbled. "What would be the point?" She swung her satchel irritably. "None, that's what. A waste of time. And why would I want to involve myself in Jonas's life? Because that's what I'd be doing." She stopped, pivoted, pivoted again.

The huddle of physicians making rounds scoped her out, decided she was probably harmless, then ignored her as they closed together in a clump of white coats and badges.

She couldn't decide why she was so torn. "Phooey," she grumbled under her breath as she fiddled with her satchel. "Come on, McDonald. Make up your mind. Time's a-wasting." Clearly her brain had turned to oatmeal, cold, congealed, clotted oatmeal. An altogether unpleasant condition.

Pacing in small circles, she gave herself a sotto voce pep talk. "You can do this, Jessie McDonald. You know you can. You're good at making decisions. You've made some swell ones. And this one is a no-brainer. Quit dithering."

Still....

She stopped.

If she went? "Jonas would think I was crazy. That's what. He'd have to. Until this week, I hadn't seen him for years. I don't know his family, and I show up, literally, on their doorstep?" Muttering, she slapped her forehead. "Duh, what in heaven am I thinking of?" She pivoted toward the elevator, then pivoted back toward Hoyt Tyler's room.

"Bad day, I guess. Need some help?" A slim brown hand carrying a stethoscope touched her arm, and mocha-brown eyes met hers. Waiting, the woman scrutinized her with concern. "Are you all right?"

"Yes. No." Jessie grimaced as she waggled her hand from side to side. "Thanks, Cara, but I'm just trying to organize my thoughts. All two of them." Oh, yes, indeedy, she needed help. But Cara couldn't help.

"Sure?" Cara smiled gently. "Not like you to be playing windshield wiper in the hall, Jessie. Or was that a new dance step you were working on?"

Jessie laughed. "Don't I wish?"

"I've been watching you for the last several minutes from the fort. I couldn't decide what the heck you were up to."

"Up to no good, probably. Aren't you on rounds? I saw the herd back that way." She waggled her hand in the general direction of the physicians she'd passed. "I'd love to visit, but don't let me keep you. Regardless of how it looks, I'm in full possession of most of my faculties."

"Whatever you say. You're over twenty-one. You ought to know if you need help." With an amused shrug, Cara touched her shoulder briefly before heading back to the fort with a long-legged stride that ate up ground and took her quickly out of sight.

Jessie headed back to the elevator.

She couldn't do this.

"No way. Uh-uh. Brain spasm, that's what this whole idea was." Her sneakers squeaked against the tile floor as she stomped down the soothing green corridor. "That's all. Misfiring brain cells. Because of all that oatmeal that's trying to pass for a brain."

Her steps slowed down as she headed toward the elevator. During the night she'd woken up several times thinking about Jonas's phone call. Disturbed by the sense that he'd reached out to her without wanting to and without consciously choosing to, compelled by some powerful need beyond his control or understanding, she'd decided on the spur of the moment to stop by his father's room. Even though Jonas had rejected her earlier offer of help, he'd phoned her during the solitary hours while he kept guard by his father's bedside.

He'd wanted something from *her*.

He'd needed a human voice in the midnight hours and he'd reached out to her, forging a connection on some emotional level that still troubled her. He'd moved past her defenses so easily, so fast, leaving her disturbed. Like a stone-hard biscuit crumbling under hot milk, her resistance had melted against the impact of his loneliness.

She didn't like that image of herself, crumbling. She'd worked hard to create Jessie McDonald, a woman who took what life and fate handed her and dealt with it. Jessie McDonald didn't wilt, fold, or crumble.

Well, she might occasionally wilt, she admitted to herself in a grumpy rush of candor. But she hadn't even put up a token resistance to the lure of Jonas Riley's voice whispering in her ear in the midnight hours, his loneliness mating with her own.

Afterward, waking up with the morning sun pouring through the window and onto her, she'd looked down at Gopher's pillow-reddened cheek, and confusion and self-doubt had engulfed her. There had been a luxurious seduction in waking up with Gopher snuggled up to her and the memory of Jonas's voice coming low and deep over the wire to her, humming inside her. There had been a sense of completeness, the three of them joined in the warmth of the morning and first waking.

But in that sleep-rumpled, sun-warmed bed, she'd been turned inside out by the questions rushing through her.

Why had she been so susceptible to Jonas after all this time? Disoriented, she'd decided she needed to find out what that moment meant, why she'd been so seduced by that illusory sense of happiness.

So she'd checked and discovered that Jonas's father had been moved out of intensive care and transferred to regular nursing care. Finishing work with the veterans on the writing pieces they were gathering for the *Stars and Stripes,* she'd headed over to the hospital.

Halfway down the hall, she flipped a mental coin.

Stay. Go.

The corridor was too short. Even so, her palms were sweaty by the time she reached the partially closed door of 630.

Hoping no one would hear her tentative rap, she knocked on the door.

"Come in." Jonas's deep voice carried over the murmur of male voices.

Poking her head carefully and apprehensively around the corner of Hoyt Tyler's door, Jessie prepared for a quick introduction and exit. Her eyes widened.

Shoulder to shoulder, three sun-burnished cowboys slouched in front of her. Their startled expressions at her appearance and their wary, narrowed gazes were almost identical as they shifted protectively and unconsciously toward the man on the bed.

"Hey there, ma'am, looking for someone?" A man with the look of Jonas and a smile that was made for tempting turned to her.

"Can we help you?" The second blond-haired man in the middle with his foot propped on the windowsill straightened and stepped closer to an older woman in a pale green linen sheath. Light filtering down onto his head turned the strands red-gold.

"Jessie?" Guarded, careful, Jonas's question increased her chagrin.

"Me." She shrugged, as uncomfortable as she'd known she'd be.

"What on earth—" He frowned.

"Friend of yours, I guess, Buck?" The brother in the middle stepped back, his expression carefully noncommittal.

"Yeah." Not moving, Jonas kept looking at her. "Friend of mine."

"Lucky you," drawled the man with the smile to tempt an angel off the straight and narrow.

Jessie swallowed and turned to Jonas. "I wanted to see how your dad was. To see if I could...I thought I might be able to help..." Her words trailed off, her brain and tongue paralyzed by the trio in front of her.

She recognized Jonas's half brothers. Even if they hadn't been in the room with him, anyone would have known these three men were related. The DNA bonding them showed in every line of their features and bodies.

"Well, ma'am, step right in." The tempter swept his arm in front of him.

"Mmm." She glanced in Jonas's direction and shrugged, her discomfort growing by the second.

Side by side, Jonas and his brothers made her think of sunshine captured in a bottle, with their shades of dark red-blond hair and brilliant blue eyes shading to blue-green. They stood the same, their rangy bodies bespeaking the kind of tough, bred-in-the-bones confidence that distinguished some men even in the cradle.

In an instinctive response to all that masculine grace and power, she ran a hand through her hair, fluffing it out. Catching her action, she grimaced, heat staining her cheeks.

"Sure. Come on in. Don't be shy." A twitch flicked the corners of the mouth of the brother who'd first offered help, and Jessie's face burned.

For heaven's sake, she'd never fluffed in her life. She wasn't a fluffy kind of woman, although she had to admit that the impact of these three men made her wish for an instant that she were a delicate flower of womanhood waiting to be swept off her feet.

No matter what she'd claimed to Jonas, once in a while a woman got tired of carrying the whole load by herself. Jonas and his brothers had a strength in their shoulders and bearing that spoke of power and stability. Good shoulders for leaning on if a woman needed a little comfort.

Not that she did, she thought, watching the tiny tightening of the lines around Jonas's eyes, the subtle tension running over his lean body as he continued to study her. She didn't need anything from Jonas. And certainly not comfort.

Even if she did, he was the last person she'd ask.

"Come to visit then, Jess?"

"Unless…I was concerned…." Stunned by the effect of these men all in one place, Jess stumbled over her thoughts, her words trailing off into silence. Hoping her glasses hadn't fogged over, she nudged them back up the bridge of her nose.

Jonas's brothers shot him a quick look, then glanced at each other and back to her, their expressions mirroring each other as they moved away, making room for her to join them, Jonas shifting as they stepped to the side.

Men like these drew a woman's gaze whether she intended it or not. They walked with that loose-hipped ease that made a woman's thoughts turn to things other than errands and patient records, reminding her of all she'd missed, like long hot nights filled with quickened breaths and urgent whispers. Men like these should come with warning labels. *Caution: Too Hot to Handle.*

Singly, each man could have sent a woman's hormones into full alert, but together—

Jessie drew in a quick breath and tried to ignore the fluttering in her stomach.

Together, the brothers could resurrect a medieval virgin with nothing more than a lopsided smile and a flash of those sea blue eyes.

She was no medieval virgin.

And it had been a very, very long time since she'd thought about hormones and hot summer nights.

Men like these made a room too small, too close, the masculine energy, even on idle, unsettling.

"Thinking it over, Jess?" Some kind of challenge whetted the edge of Jonas's question.

She tugged at the long loop of her gold earring.

"Promise we won't bite if you risk it," teased the brother with the melt-a-girl-into-butter smile.

"Zip it up, Hattie," advised Jonas's other brother as Jonas sent them a hard look.

Oh, there were differences among the men. What she noticed most was that Jonas seemed part of them, yet not quite. His eyes were a deeper, stormier blue, his frame a little leaner and broader in the shoulders, the lines around his eyes not quite the same kind of laugh lines his brothers wore. Like summer lightning snapping distantly on the horizon, an aura of excitement crackled around him.

Unlike his brothers, Jonas was not a comfortable man.

"Buck, we're minding our manners, but I think you're scaring your friend off. Sorry, ma'am, ol' Buck forgets how to behave sometimes." The brother she'd picked out as the youngest, the one they'd called Hattie, shook his head regretfully, his eyes sparkling with devilment.

But it was Jonas to whom her gaze returned, Jonas on whom her eyes lingered. She'd always liked walking on the edge, and the undercurrents running deep and dangerous in Jonas spoke to a matching side of her nature.

"You might as well come on in, Jessie," he drawled, his glance speculative. "Quit hemming and hawing."

"Oh, that's good cowboy lingo," she said admiringly, surfacing for air and finding her voice.

Standing next to the window, her back to Jessie, their mother turned to her. "I'm sorry. I was lost in my thoughts." She smiled, a delicate, feminine version of the masculine megawatt smiles of her sons.

"Mama, may I introduce a...former colleague, Jessie McDonald? We worked together for a while at Collins, Keane and Riley. She works at the hospital now and I do believe she's come to offer comfort and assistance.'' An irony Jessie knew was intended only for her ears colored his comment.

Ignoring him, his mother spoke to her. "Hello, Ms. McDonald—''

"Jessie. Please.'' She took a step forward, regretting with every click of the clock on the wall the whim that had brought her up to the sixth floor.

"Certainly. And call me Bea. Come in.''

"As I said, I don't want to intrude—'' Retreating into formality, Jessie didn't look at Jonas, but from the corner of her eye, she saw him fold his arms across his chest and step back, his brothers making room for him, even as she took another step forward. Rejection didn't come much more clearly expressed, she thought grimly, her feet carrying her forward through sludge pits while her brain kept shrieking, *Stop! Stop!*

"I've probably come at a bad time—''

"No, not in the least. Anyway, you know how hospitals are. Privacy doesn't exist. Everybody's been waltzing in and out all morning since Hoyt was moved from the ICU. Blood counts, temperature checks. Everyone's real helpful, but *that's* intrusion. A friendly face come to visit is no intrusion.'' Bea Tyler waved her forward.

"He's doing better?''

"Hoyt's sleeping right now, a real sleep. That's a relief.'' Bea's face went blank as she turned to her husband, and a prickle of uneasiness skittered down Jessie's back.

She caught sight of the man behind the half-drawn curtain before she lowered her eyes. There was privacy and *privacy*. She wouldn't want anyone staring at her while she was asleep. "It's a good sign they moved him so quickly,'' she said, feeling her way.

"Actually, some poor lady was admitted who needed the bed worse than Hoyt did at the moment since the bleeding had finally been brought under control. We're grateful Hoyt's out of intensive care.''

"This is a good hospital,'' Jessie added. "Good people. They're pretty straightforward around here. You can trust them.''

"Oh, yes. I can tell that." Bea's glance drifted to Jonas, her face growing momentarily empty before her glance returned to her husband lying on the bed.

Jessie wished she could add more, could give this woman with her sweet smile and steely core some genuine assurance that her husband would be better, but offering false encouragement seemed cruel, particularly in light of the way Bea had controlled her reaction so carefully. Her emotions and reactions seemed a bit too carefully reined in, Jessie thought. But what did she know? That might be Bea Tyler's personality.

But the tiny prickles of uneasiness increased the more Jessie watched the other woman, so she said, "It's a good place to be. If you have to be in a hospital," she added and averted her gaze from Jonas's tight face.

"Hoyt doesn't like hospitals."

"Nobody does."

"Too much noise and confusion. I don't know how in the world a body could be expected to sleep—" her voice trembled "—well, we'll be happier when we can take him home."

"I hope that'll be soon?" Jessie rested her satchel on the floor. Oh, she should have listened to the little voice telling her she was making a mistake.

"We don't know—" Bea turned first to Jonas, and then shrugged her shoulders as Hank and T.J. remained silent. Her face was a softer, blurred version of the angled sharpness of her sons. While all three men showed the strength of her imprint, Jonas resembled her the least.

"What Mama's saying is that we don't know anything yet about what caused the bleeding. The test results haven't come in." Jonas's expression was neutral, concealing his thoughts and reminding her of his mother's control, but even so, his gaze skimmed over Jessie, over her legs and hips in a quick, unconscious checking-out that set her stomach fluttering again as he said, "I'm fairly sure Daddy's going to be here a while."

"I'm—sorry to hear that." Pressing her hand to her forehead, Jessie smoothed out the frown. She didn't like the sound of that, but she kept silent. She'd butted in. It wasn't her place to react to what she thought she heard in the silences between Jonas's comments.

Propping himself casually against the wall, he said, "So, Jessie, you had some free time in your busy life and stopped to visit, huh?"

Jessie nodded. Her braid slid across the back of her bare shoulders, tickling her, and Jonas's gaze followed the brush of braid against the skin of her bare arm. Her skin tightened as if it had been the back of his hand that brushed lightly over her. "I was on my way home." She had another stop, but this room wasn't the place to discuss where she was headed next. "I had a few extra minutes."

"You might as well meet the clan, then." With a cursory gesture, he indicated the matching set of blue-shirted, jeans-clad cowboys. "These two reprobates are, first, my middle brother, Thomas Jefferson, T.J. to most everybody, and, next, Hank, the rascal of the Tyler family."

"Rascal, Buck? That a case of the old pot calling the kettle black, or are you jealous of my youth and handsomeness?" Casting Jessie a look filled with guile and veiled intelligence, Hank continued, "See, Buck truly does believe that no one knows about his dirty linen, so the rest of us play along with him, seeing as how he's so ancient and we don't want to raise his blood pressure. We're thoughtful that way because we love the old scudder in spite of his argumentative tendencies and wicked ways."

Mischief and good humor dazzled Jessie, making her catch her breath. Hank Tyler was a heartbreaker. *Rascal* was a good term for him.

T.J. dipped his head. "Nice to meet you, Ms. Jessie McDonald. Any friend of Buck's, et cetera." A gold wedding band flashed as he ran his hand through his hair, the dark gold strands gleaming even in the muted light of the hospital room. He studied her for a second, then sent a thoughtful look Jonas's way. Then, as he returned his brilliant gaze to her, his eyes narrowed intently. Suddenly, as if he'd reached some conclusion, he nodded, devilment dancing in his eyes.

Jessie had all she could do not to blush. T.J.'s impact, while quieter, was as powerful, more like Jonas's, but without Jonas's edgy element.

The three of them must have been a handful for Bea Tyler during their teenage years, but their support of her and their father was tender, affecting in the automatic way their attention focused on Bea and Hoyt even as they teased Jessie.

She couldn't help smiling back at T.J. and Hank. They were irresistible flirts, and they knew it. "So this is what I can expect in a few decades when my son grows up?"

"Decades, ma'am? A few?" T.J.'s sly smile lifted one side of his mouth. "You wound me." He laid his hand across his heart.

"You wear your decades well," Jessie said demurely. "I congratulate you."

T.J. raised his hands out and flashed his version of that killer Tyler smile. "Ouch. But I should have known any friend of Buck's from his lawyering days couldn't resist a battle of wits—"

"Nope." Jonas interrupted. "Jessie fights fair. She'd never fight an unarmed opponent."

"Ignore them," Bea counseled Jessie with a wave of her hand. "They tend to get out of hand even though they're old enough to know better. I think the boys are getting a little rambunctious because Hoyt's feeling better." Even though Bea was teasing her sons in much the same way they'd teased each other, her too-bright smile troubled Jessie.

Experience with enough patients and their families had taught Jessie to listen to her inner voice, and she focused closely on the older woman, observing the interplay between her and her trio of tall sons.

"Boys, Mama?" Hank laid his arm over Bea's much shorter shoulders.

"To me, always." Bea's smile was tender, as protective in its way as Hank's, as she tipped her head up to her son and patted his beard-shaded cheek.

"Aw, Ma, you're a cutie-pie, you are." Hank's noisy kiss reminded Jessie of Gopher's enthusiastic kisses.

She could tell that, for Bea, her sons would always remain

boys in her heart, no matter how old either she or they became. For Bea, that cord between mother and child might be stretched, but never snapped.

In that moment, and in spite of everything, Jess envied Jonas's mother with all her heart. Families might be a foreign country to her, but she wished she could visit a while in the country of the Tylers. "You're a lucky woman, Bea, to have your sons with you."

"That I am." Bea linked her arm through Jonas's.

Seeing Bea with her sons, Jessie envied her and wanted that same kind of relationship for herself and Gopher. She yearned to give him that kind of family continuity through the years, the confidence that came from knowing no matter what happened, you *could* go home again, that there was a place where you'd always be welcome, no matter how you had failed.

She hadn't had that sense of her own special place in the world.

But Gopher would. No matter what she had to do, her son was not going to be shortchanged. She'd learn the language and territory of families if it killed her.

An unwelcome and disturbing realization struck Jessie as she caught the exchange of glances between Jonas and his brothers. Gopher had no one except her. His entire family was made up of Jessie and whoever she brought into the closed circle of their lives, like Lolly.

Like Jessie, Gopher would never share that richness of emotion Jonas shared with the people in this room. And if anything happened to her— Had she made an enormous mistake, an error of pride and judgment that could damage her son, cheat him? Pride could be a destructive emotion. As the thought froze her, she glimpsed Jonas's frown. Stricken, she avoided his probing gaze.

She had to get out of this room. She grabbed her satchel and let words, any words, tumble out. "It was lovely meeting all of you, but I have to go." She shoved a piece of paper that had worked its way free of the stack back inside her bag. "I have another stop to make on my way out, but, please, don't hesitate to call if I can do anything at all, will you? I'm familiar with the hospital, the routine, the people. Call me. Anytime. I wouldn't mind, okay?''

"I might." Straightening the thermal cover, Bea peeked at her husband, fiddling with the sheet, her fingers trailing over the shape of his shoulder. "I might do that."

Hoyt stirred under the cover, and murmured something Jessie didn't hear. As she turned away, she met Bea Tyler's eyes. And in that instant as the two women stared at each other, a terrible knowledge passed from the older woman to Jessie.

Stunned, she couldn't speak.

Jonas's mother's eyes held an awful truth that sucked Jessie's breath away, leaving her cold.

The reports on Hoyt's condition hadn't come in; the doctors hadn't given Bea a diagnosis or prognosis. It didn't matter. On an instinctive level, a level beyond reason and logic, Bea knew that Hoyt was more ill than anyone was telling her at this point. Whatever the physicians said to her in the next few days would only confirm Bea Tyler's intuition.

The subconscious signals that had been making Jessie apprehensive had come from Bea, from the woman's efforts to hide from her sons the truth she suspected. With her bag in her hands, Jessie hesitated. There was nothing she could say or do. And so much she wanted to do. To say. She reached out her hand, let it drop to her side. Oh, she was lousy at this, never knowing exactly what to say, to do. The thought might count, but, as the proverbial "they" were fond of saying, actions spoke louder than words. And she'd never known quite how to act at moments like these.

Bea didn't want to burden Hank, T.J. and Jonas with her awareness.

Fumbling for the handle of her satchel, distress making her awkward, Jessie saw Jonas go motionless. His gaze met hers and the handle slipped through her fingers.

Jonas, too, knew.

Oh, Jonas, she thought, understanding finally the undercurrent of desolation running through him.

Buck saw the change in her face, the thoughts flickering through her eyes. "I thought you were through for the day?"

he asked, letting a little aggression show, anything to wipe that stricken expression off Jessie's face, anything so that he wouldn't have to acknowledge that look.

She shook her head, momentarily dazed. "For all intents and purposes, I am. I have one more stop I wanted to make. In pediatrics."

"I'll walk you to the elevator."

"No, really, don't." She pushed her glasses up her narrow nose again, her forehead wrinkling as she answered. "I'll see you all later. Take care." She was already at the door, her braid swinging from side to side across her back, blond strands blending with the nothing-colored jacket.

"As a thank-you. For stopping in." He strolled toward her, made his walk carefully casual. The misery and compassion in her face unnerved him.

"Really, that's not necessary."

"I could use some fresh air." He needed to move, to unleash the low-down mean misery boiling in him. He couldn't handle her compassion, her sympathy, not in this room with its weight of unspoken knowledge. "Back in a minute, folks. Okay?"

"Sure. No objections here." The twitch at the corner of T.J.'s mouth spoke volumes. Twenty years ago, that twitch would have sent both of them wrestling to the floor.

"Take your time, Buck. You have to be tired. You were here all day."

"No, Mama." He turned to her, and she squeezed his hand. "I'm not tired. It'll only be a minute or two."

What Jessie thought she knew, Buck had no idea, but he was afraid she'd seen his reactions and drawn her own conclusions.

Jessie had always been a real whiz at drawing conclusions. And he reckoned he'd like it a whole lot better if she didn't apply that clever intelligence of hers to his situation.

When he swiveled back to the door, she'd disappeared, a wisp of that coffee-cream material that was neither skirt nor shorts flicking out of sight. "T.J., if y'all need me before I'm back, page me." He gestured toward the pager at his waist.

He couldn't talk with Hank or T.J. about what he suspected, what he feared his mother believed. Maybe Jessie had talked to the nurses and picked up information that hadn't been passed on to him. Anyway, the room had been closing in on him during the past two hours. He needed to clear his head, or he'd go stark-staring nuts.

He could have come up with fifty more reasons to follow her.

But the most powerful one was that he wanted to.

She moved fast.

Eventually he found her on the pediatric oncology floor.

Huddled on the floor outside a room decorated with cutout balloons and cloudy pink angels, she was bent over, facing away from him, her arms wrapped around her head. The satchel that was almost as big as a suitcase lay beside her, loose papers and cellophane-wrapped packages of tissues visible through its opening.

Moving slowly, he approached her, wondering what had brought her to the highly glossed floor. With her back to him, she didn't hear him as he came up beside her. Curious, he looked inside the room, his shoulder brushing one of the shiny angels.

The name on the placard read Kelly Marie.

Aw, hell, he thought, as he glanced into the room.

On the narrow white bed with its raised metal sides, a child lay sleeping, her warm pink gown a blush against the sheet. Without the name on the door, he wouldn't have known she was a little girl. Against the pillow, her smooth, pale scalp was androgynous, a lovely, curving shape. Her face was puffy and round, the moon-shape of drug therapy.

Curled under her thin arm, Skeezix lay next to her. Lifting his shaggy head as Buck stayed there, the dog's eyes met his with canine intelligence. Skeezix thumped his plumed tail twice gently against the bed. Whispering something to the dog and snuggling closer, Kelly Marie dug her fingers into Skeezix's fur and tightened her grip.

Turning away, Buck took a deep breath as he looked down at the thick richness of Jessie's braid resting against her shaking shoulders. He understood why it was pulled back into that tight, controlled braid. "Jess?"

She didn't answer.

"Hey, kiddo, look at me." Holding out a package of the tissues he'd filched from her bag, he hunkered down, facing her.

Her head jerked up. Hot and dry, her eyes burned through him. "I'm not crying. I don't cry. Ever." Her eyes glittered, but she'd told the truth. She wasn't crying. There were no tear tracks down her square face, no shine of tears on her skin.

He reached out to touch her shoulder, to comfort her. Or maybe he needed the touch of another person himself.

Shoving her hands out in front of her, palms up, she glared at him. "Don't touch me."

"What?"

Her face was white, fierce. "Don't touch me. I mean it," she continued as he stared at her.

"I'm sorry, Jess." Ignoring her words, hearing the pain she denied, he smoothed his knuckle against a strand of hair that had come loose from her braid, tucking the curl back into place. "Here." He pulled a tissue free and stuck it under her nose.

"Just go away. Leave me alone. Please." She lowered her head, and the tissue fluttered to her lap. "Go away, Jonas."

"I don't think I can do that."

"Jonas, for God's sake, go away!" The huskiness of her voice dipped and wavered, cracked. "Please!"

But of course he couldn't. How could he? Leave her with the immensity of what was happening mere feet away in that hospital room? Abandon her to this dry grief blazing through her as if it were a prairie fire? "C'mon, Jess." He cupped her elbows, lifting her with him as he stood up. "C'mon."

A faint trembling ran through her, a minute and continuous rippling he felt through the tips of his fingers against her skin, that trembling shaking her to bits inside, and yet she didn't, wouldn't, shed a tear. "I'm sorry, Jess. This has to be hard." Tucking her head against him, he enclosed her in his arms, his touch having nothing to do with lust or sex or with anything except the need to comfort her, comfort himself, to hold someone during this walk through the shadowed valley. "Shh, shh," he said, running his open palms over the long curve of her spine. "Shh, sweetheart." He didn't tell her everything would be okay. She was too smart for lies.

"Damn you," she whispered, sagging against him. "Damn you, Jonas. I don't cry." An ugly sound ripped through her, and her forehead banged against his chest. Her fingers scrabbled over his shirt. "I told you, I *told* you to go away. Why wouldn't you listen to me?" she said in such a raw, low voice that he scarcely heard her. "I wanted you to leave me alone." Tears trembled on her lashes.

With a quick scoop, he snagged her satchel, and urged her down the hall, away from prying eyes, until he found an empty alcove where two walls made an L of privacy. Turning his back to the hall, he shielded her from passersby. "I didn't realize. This is what you do?" He gestured back down the hall. "This is pet therapy?"

With her head down, her voice flat in that way truth always came out, no dramatics, only that emotionless, distanced recitation that he'd learned came when the speaker was wounded too deeply for words, she said, "Kelly hasn't been sleeping. Her treatment has been painful. She needs sleep. She forgets how much she hurts when the animals are with her. She plays with them. They help her forget. Then she sleeps. When one of them stays. Loofah. Skeezix. They help her sleep."

As long as he lived, Buck would never forget that small, frail hand fisted into Skeezix's fur.

He didn't want to know what the future held for Kelly Marie.

She was sleeping. She wasn't in pain. That was enough. "You work with the children, too? As well as with the vets?" His mouth was dry.

Jessie nodded, her nose bumping the middle button of his shirt. She shuddered against him, her small, sturdy frame fragile in the wrench of all that cruel emotion, all those unshed tears burning in her glittering eyes as she looked up at him. Her voice was the scraped sound of ripping fabric as she said,

"You should have left me alone, Jonas. It would have been better. I don't want a shoulder to cry on. I don't need comforting."

"I know you don't. You told the truth, Jess. You don't cry. You don't need a shoulder to lean against. You're a woman of the nineties. I can see that, and God knows I'm not offering you a shoulder. Or support. I'm just standing here in the hall with you, Jess, that's all. Nothing more. A friend. Standing in the hall with another old friend." He ran his hand over the slippery rope of her braided hair and tugged, gently, until she bowed her head, and he lowered his chin on top of her silky scalp, bringing her so close to him that her shudders trembled through him and that rich scent of her hair and skin filled him, easing the tight band around his heart. "I know you don't need a shoulder to lean on, Jess. But maybe I do. Maybe I do."

Chapter Six

As Jessie's arms crept around his waist, holding him as tightly as he held her, Buck drew in a shuddering breath. The ugly sounds coming from her were painful, dry sobs finally giving way to tears as she clung to him.

He didn't know how long she wept against him, her arms locked around him. Hours, days. Half his lifetime. It didn't matter. Holding her, letting her tears baptize him, in those moments he felt at peace, all the wound-up tension uncoiling inside him and loosening its tentacles. He couldn't explain the solace touching her gave him, but it entered him as if it were a benediction. He could have stayed in that curious sanctuary of shared touch, breathing in the scent of her, not thinking, forever.

When the sobs shaking her died away, she kept her face buried into his shirt.

"When was the last time you cried, Jess?"

"Not since—" She rubbed her wet cheek against his shirt, and plucked at the damp material. "I've ruined your shirt. And you've been wearing it for *days*." Tears seeped out of her swollen eyes. "You need a new shirt, Jonas." Tears dripped down her nose and cheeks. "You used to have the most beautiful clothes!'' Fretfully, she fanfolded the wet fabric until it was a wad of cloth. ''I *loved* your suits, Jonas. And now I've ruined your only shirt.''

Yanking the edge of his shirt free, he wiped her face dry. ''I'll send you a bill, Jess. You can buy me a new one.''

''I will.'' She rubbed her forehead back and forth across his shirt. ''I promise.'' One final shiver rippled through her. Her rigid grip loosened. She stepped backward, breaking the contact between them and making room for the cold meanness to ooze its way back inside him.

Clipping her arms to his sides, he said, ''Wait.'' He didn't want to turn her loose, to let her walk away from him down the hall and out to her car. ''Jess, how do you do your job every day, how do you face this?'' With his chin he indicated the hospital halls, the rooms. ''The weight of all this hope. How do you bear it?''

His shirt was soaked, plastered against him in spots, and her voice was still raspy with tears. ''These kids bear it. I can. And when I go home, I leave it behind me. They can't walk away from any of what faces them. I can. I make their struggle easier, that's all. The weight's all on them. Not me,'' she said fiercely. ''My part's easy.''

''I see. Tears are a sign of weakness, Jess?''

She glared at him. ''Of course not. People cry all the time.''

''People. But not Jessie McDonald, right?'' If he kept her talking, arguing, she would stay. He wouldn't be alone. He knew he was being selfish, and he didn't want to analyze the reasons that made him try to keep her by his side. All he knew was that he wanted her there, right there beside him in these green-painted halls. He needed her when he'd never needed anyone before in his life. ''Accepting comfort makes *you* a weaker person?''

''I don't know. But you shouldn't have followed me, Jonas. I won't insult their courage by falling apart, so don't tempt me, do you hear? I don't have time or energy for collapsing in a heap at somebody else's feet.'' Even with her arms around him, she shook him, her damp, reddened face lifting to his. ''So don't give me sympathy I don't want, don't need and can't afford. All right?'' She snapped her head back, and the end of her braid flipped up, down, whipped against his hand.

"Who comforts you in the dark hours?'' He had a feeling Jessie McDonald didn't allow much comforting. "Is comfort subversive, Jess? Does accepting it undermine your independence? You won't accept sympathy, comfort, or a helping hand. What *do* you need, Jess?''

"What do I need? Nothing.'' She stepped away from him and stooped to lift her satchel. "I have everything I need. My son. My job.'' She checked her watch. "Speaking of which, I'm late.'' Hoisting the satchel over her shoulder, she threw him a challenging glance. "What about you, Jonas? What do you need?''

He crossed his arms. Surprising him, the admission slipped out. "Like I said, maybe a shoulder to lean on.''

She sighed. "I'm not that shoulder, Jonas. I can't be. I'm no good at—comforting.''

"Too bad.'' He sketched a line in the air, skimming past her chin, down her neck, past the curve of her shoulder. The barely visible hairs on her arm rose in the wake of his imaginary line and, even not touching her, he could feel the heat of her skin as he passed his hand in the air over her. "And a very nice shoulder it is, too, Jess, but I wasn't talking about sex, you know. Have to say, though, I sure do like the way your mind works. So if you want to—talk about sex, that is—I'm willing. I mean, a cowpoke's gotta do what a cowpoke's gotta do. Code of the West.'' He shot her his most virtuous, accommodating look. "So go right ahead.''

She shook her head, her expression pitying as she waved her hand dismissively. "Whatever. Do you flirt in your sleep, Jonas? I ask because you do it so unconsciously. I think.''

"Now, Jess,'' he chided, "what would be the point of flirting in my sleep? Besides, I don't flirt.''

"No? What would you call it?''

"Making conversation,'' he said and smiled at her strangled sound of exasperation. "Two friends, talking.''

"Thanks for clarifying that for me.'' She walked toward the juncture of the hall, and just before turning down the corridor to the elevator, she stopped, her expression troubled. Hesitating, she added, "I'm so sorry about Hoyt."

His throat tightening, he nodded.

"Even though he's out of intensive care, he's not doing well, is he?" Her fingers looped in and out of the strap of her satchel.

"What makes you think so? Did one of the nurses talk to you?"

"Of course not." The matte skin of her forehead wrinkled. "They wouldn't." As she faced him, she hugged the satchel to her. "Your mother knows, doesn't she?"

"I think so."

"I hope—"

"Yeah. Me too." He took one step sideways, another step in the opposite direction. He'd thought he didn't want to talk about Hoyt, but Jess was there in front of him, her face glowing with a concern that slipped under his defenses and shone in the dark corners of his heart. "We haven't discussed the situation."

"Then why—" She stopped. "I'm sorry. I've already butted in enough for one day." She darted left at the same moment he moved, bumping up against him.

Once more he cupped the sharp points of her elbows in his hands. "Yes, you're butting in. But I don't mind. You were going to ask me why I think Daddy's situation is serious?"

She nodded, her braid flipping over her shoulder to the front, the end curling toward her neck and a small freckle that showed above her pink collar. He wanted to take the curl and draw it over her skin, connect that freckle with other, unseen ones.

"During the night, when he's awake, he—he talks to me. He's worried about Mama. He keeps telling me to take care of her. To take care of the boys—" He shook his head. "*The boys!* Hell, T.J.'s almost thirty-eight, Hank's thirty-five. He wants me to look after them. He keeps talking about that, about taking care of everybody. About grandchildren." Restless, Buck paced the other way. "He wants to see all the kids.

Like Flynn-to-be, Hank and Jilly's baby. She's due in September.''

It was a relief to talk to Jessie after all, to let out everything he couldn't say to his mother or to his brothers. "Daddy talks like—well—'' He slapped the wall with his fist. "I can't explain it. He's different. There's a look in his eyes that ties knots inside me.''

Jessie touched him briefly, her finger sliding down his sleeve to rest at his wrist. "As if he's listening to something only he can hear?''

"Yeah. Like that. Like he hears a voice way off in the distance telling him something that none of the rest of us can follow.''

"Perhaps he is, Jonas.'' She started to remove her hand.

Covering it with his, he lifted it, turned it over. "Strong hands, Jessie.'' He traced the callus on her palm, the one along the edge. "Beautiful hands.''

Her smile was self-conscious as she tugged at his grip and, reluctantly, he released her. "Not quite the same style as when I worked at Collins, Keane and Riley.''

"No.'' He liked her work-roughened palms. Their combination of vulnerability and strength drew him. He held out his own scarred and toughened hands. "Not quite the same style, either.''

With her index finger she traced the thin white scar left by the tip of a bull's horn, her thumb moving along the curve of his thumb to the outside of his wrist. "You work hard, don't you? On your ranch?''

"Yeah. Sometimes.''

One silky eyebrow elevated, but she didn't say anything for a moment, continuing to follow the lines of old scars, her touch soothing as if she could heal old wounds. Then, with her head bowed over his hand, she asked, "Jonas? What does Hoyt say about you?''

Trust Jessie to hit the nail on the head. Like a magnet pointing due north, she'd settled dead-on to what was tearing him apart.

"Because he's worried about you, too, isn't he?''

"Yeah, I reckon," he said reluctantly.

"And?" Her thumb rested lightly against his scars as her gaze held his, that limpid blue restful, the blaze of fire gone. "Who's to look after you, Jonas?"

"You think I need looking after, Jess?" He gave a spin to the words, turning the seriousness of her question aside. Like her, he could skirt issues with the best of them.

"But it's not what I think, is it?" Her smile was gentle. "What's bothering Hoyt about you and your life, Jonas?"

"He keeps insisting...he thinks I need— Well, it's not important." He couldn't tell her about those rambling conversations that left him wrung out.

"He's worried because Hank and T.J. are settled with families of their own, and you don't have anyone."

"Hell, Jess." He spun away. "You running a little mind-reading scam on the side?" She'd left him feeling naked, and he didn't like it. "My life's the way I want it. I told you that."

"Actually you talked about a midlife crisis and a biological clock, Jonas. That clock being yours, as I recall. And you mentioned that possibly ranching wasn't exactly what you'd thought it would be. Remember?"

"Yeah, now that you bring it up." He stuffed his hands into his pockets.

"Does that sound to you like someone whose life is the way he wants it to be?" That damned eyebrow zipped up, and the tiny smile curling the edge of her mouth was a shade too self-satisfied.

"No, Jess, I reckon it doesn't. And I reckon my daddy's worried that I'm turning into one of those old bachelor cowboys that squat on the front stoop of the country store and spit tobaccy into the dirt." He strode back toward her, passed, turned. "There." He flung his arms wide. "That what you wanted to hear?"

"You spitting—tobaccy?" she asked innocently. "Interesting picture." Her face was prim. "*Is* there a country store down in Okeechobee, Jonas? Even in your wet, well-worn shirt, I'm having difficulty imagining you that casual."

"Smart mouth." He tapped her chin. He knew what she

was doing. As fast as she could, she was trying to make him forget that moment when she'd revealed what was to her a weakness.

"Are you turning into one of those old Southern bachelors, Jonas? Living out in the country, eating raw gator and coming into town only when you have to?"

"That prospect's becoming more attractive by the minute, Jessie."

"And why would that be, Jonas? Am I getting on your nerves?" The bite of lemon in all the honeyed sweetness of her voice was pure Jessie. She passed him, the satchel smacking against his thigh. If he were a betting man, he'd reckon that smack wasn't accidental.

"Yes and no. But I like having you zing 'em right back to me. Problem is, we're too much alike, Jess, did you know that?" He followed her to the elevator, giving the satchel a generous berth.

"And how would that be?" She jiggled her wrist, flicked the face of her watch. "Please tell me. You have my undivided attention. At least until the elevator comes." Her jittery movements recalled the Jessica he'd known years ago.

"You're angry with me because I saw you cry. You think that gives me an advantage over you."

"And?" She checked her watch again.

"And you cut too close to the bone with your comment that T.J. and Hank are settled and I don't have anyone. What ticked me off was the feeling that you'd stepped inside my brain and read it, putting me at a disadvantage."

Once more she skirted the central issue. She jabbed the elevator button. "I shouldn't have said that. You have a lot of 'someones' in your life. You have your family, Jonas. They're crazy about you. You're the one they look up to. Even your mama does. I wonder if you have any idea how they tune in to your reactions?"

"I suppose they do."

"It's as though they're waiting, oh, not more than half a second probably, because T.J. and Hank don't strike me as men who'd wait too long for someone, even you, to take the lead." She lifted her watch to her ear, shook it again. "But, Jonas, they wait. That should make you stop and think about your place in your family."

"Is this a little free counseling on your part, now? You're balancing accounts between us?"

"Of course not. I'm sharing my observations, that's all. Make what you want to out of them." Her clear-eyed glance held an unwanted understanding.

Reacting, knowing he was trying to shift the balance between them, he said, "You have the key to my family, is that it, Jess?" No sooner had he said the words than he wished them back. Thrust and parry, thrust and parry. She saw him too clearly. He understood her too well. "You meet them once, and you think you can pinpoint what my family's like? Congratulations, Jess."

"What I know about your family or any family would almost fill a thimble, Jonas, if anyone still uses those anymore. But I observe. I'm good at that. What I observed is that you're a central focus in your family, but you make a point of floating around on the edge."

"I have no idea what you're talking about." Buck crossed his arms and leaned against the wall. "As you said, you're good at observations, but you might want to check your addition. You're adding three and two and getting six, sweetheart."

"Very nice, Jonas, that 'sweetheart' bit. Perhaps a shade too defensive, though, don't you think? A tad—snippy?" She patted his arm consolingly. "Or don't guys ever get 'snippy'? That's reserved for those of us in the feminine persuasion?"

"You know, Jess, you're something special, you are." Mixed with the irritation was dark humor. Her mix of asperity and intelligence intrigued him. He slouched against the wall, giving her his best I-don't-give-a-damn twitch of the mouth.

She looked him up and down. "The body language is good, too, Jonas. Casual, unconcerned. But you forget I studied your every case, your style, your whole presentation during those years at the law firm. I know how you operate, Jonas."

"Really? How interesting." He smiled but it took more effort than he'd admit to anyone. "That you studied me. Should I take that as a compliment, Jess?"

"Take it however you want." She headed for the exit. "I'm tired of waiting for this dratted elevator. I'm taking the stairs." As she pushed the fire door open, she paused.

Sounds came up the stairwell. An ambulance wailing in the distance. A child's wail.

Then she spoke. "I wouldn't dare hazard a guess as to why you keep yourself a bit separated from your family, but that's what I saw. And I think that part of what's going on in your head—pardon me, Jonas, for taking a stroll through your brain, of course—is that your father's worried about you, about your living just on the other side of the fence, so to speak. Now that's absolutely all I care to say. I don't have time to play games with you."

Her cheeks were flushed. With anger, with the heat of her speech, he didn't know, but she hadn't spared him. She'd fired both barrels. Jessie had always spoken the truth as she saw it, flat out. Nothing wishy-washy about her. And now he reckoned she deserved as much of an explanation as he could give her. Running his hand through his hair, scraping it back, he strode over to her, and clamped his fingers around the edge of the door. "Hold on a minute—"

"If you call me 'little missy' the way you did the other night, I swear I'll slam the door on your fingers, Jonas. Turn me loose." She pulled at the door.

"Jess, I've no intention of calling you that, but will you give me a second? I've had a lot on my mind—"

"That's more than a second."

"And none of it's your problem. It's mine. I've been on edge for a while, maybe ever since Hank and Jilly got married. I don't know why, but I've been—churned up, I guess, is the best way to explain what's been happening in my head. And now, with Daddy sick and worrying about seeing all of us settled, I—" He hit the doorknob with his fist. "You were right. I feel—pressured. To follow in Hank and T.J.'s boot steps. To march to the same drumbeat."

"And you've never liked following anybody's trail, have you? Much less staying in lockstep?"

"No."

"Besides, you prefer being footloose and fancy-free. No chains, no ties. Nobody to answer to except yourself."

"I don't know that I'd describe my philosophy that way. I'm not exactly a loner."

Her face was sad. "Jonas, I'm a very good observer. I saw how you managed to keep out of sticky romantic situations when we were working together. I don't know why you've avoided long-term relationships, but you do. I can understand you're feeling pressured now by Hoyt's illness and his compulsion to see that his affairs are taken care of, that the people he loves will be all right, later." She took a breath that lifted her rib cage and his gaze followed the lovely roundness of her breasts as they rose under the shiny pink of her blouse. "But that's between you and him. Perhaps when—when his situation is more stable, you can tell him how you feel?"

"Maybe." Distracted by the shimmer of pink and not able to put in words the lost-at-sea feeling inside him, he released the door and leaned against the wall. He was so tired he thought he could stay right there, melting into the peaceful green. Maybe that was all that was wrong with him. Too many sleepless nights over too long a period of time. Maybe a couple of nights of sleep would solve all the turmoil inside him. "I've been thinking too much about a lot of things, that's all. Running into you at the Palmetto put a sharper edge on what's eating at me, I guess. And then Daddy's illness brought everything to a head. I'm cranky, irritable and not a nice person these days. I'm about as sweet as a junkyard dawg, Jess, so just shoot me and put me out of my misery."

"That bad, is it?" she commiserated with a reluctant smile.

"Not quite, but I don't like what I see in the mirror lately."

"Take another look, Jonas," she advised. "It's not a junkyard dog looking back at you."

"What, then?"

"A man who's at a turning point."

"That's what you see?"

"It's not my opinion that counts, Jonas. Yours is the only one that matters. I've learned that, if nothing else, during these years. Think about it. Figure out what *you* want out of your life. Nobody can answer that except you."

"Easy words, Jess."

"The truth always is." Her clear gaze held his for a long moment that trembled between them with possibilities, with hazy ghosts.

The rumble of the elevator rising slowly from the basement and up through the floors vibrated against the bottom of his boots. "Come on, Jess, the elevator's here. Slow as Christmas, but it's on its way. No sense walking down all those flights now."

"I suppose not." She came back into the hall slowly. "Jonas, do you think it's possible for you and me to have a conversation that doesn't involve scoring points off each other or turning a simple interaction into an interrogation?"

"Well, you heard Hank, Jess, with his dig about my being argumentative. So, to answer your question, I'm not sure it is possible for us to have a normal conversation. There's too much going on between us. Text and subtext."

"Good that we're not working together anymore, then, isn't it?" She shifted the bag with its load of papers and tissues.

"See, Jess, how hard it is to yield, to give? We both like to be in control, and when the balance of power shifts, we retreat to zingers, jokes. Anything to keep ourselves from having to deal with whatever's going on beneath the surface. Like you said, maybe even some flirting on my part. But haven't you been flirting a little with me, too?"

"Have I?"

"See, Jessie, we both like dueling, each trying to get the upper hand, and there's all this unresolved energy between us. It has to come out somehow, whether it's in the form of one-upmanship, or jokes or flirting. That's my nature. Yours, too, if you'll be honest with yourself."

She shook her head. "Lord help me if Gopher takes after me, then. I suppose if there's any justice, he will. That would serve me right, wouldn't it?" Her face was strained. "I guess you're right. We are twin peas in a pod. That thought's enough to give me nightmares.''

"Not me. I kind of enjoy seeing what it takes to strike sparks off you, to rile you up a little. You're a worthy opponent, Jess, because you give as good as you get. You're not easy to score points off. You still look like a brisk wind would send you feet over fanny, but you're a tough cookie.''

"That's reassuring,'' she muttered. "I'd hate to get a reputation as being 'easy.''' The glance she shot him was uneasy, embarrassed, her eyes flicking up to the elevator floor display.

The light above the elevator doors seemed stuck on the fourth floor, and he wondered if she'd head down the stairwell after all. "You don't have to worry. Don't you know what your nickname was?''

"I don't think I want to know.''

"Ice Lady.''

"What?'' Her chin shot up. A storm cloud flashed through her eyes as she stared him down.

"Yeah. Because you made it so clear that you weren't interested in dating any of the lawyers in the firm and that you didn't have time to waste on extracurricular activities. Everybody knew you came back in the evenings and worked until midnight or later.''

"I didn't realize everyone knew my schedule.'' Pain flickered across her face, puzzling him. Jess wouldn't let a silly nickname hurt her, at least the Jessica he'd known wouldn't have. She would have laughed it off and found a way to turn the joke back on whoever had made up the name.

Not wanting to cause her more pain, though, he explained. "Actually, Jess, the nickname was a compliment to your commitment.''

"I see. A compliment, was it?'' Pain disappeared, leaving in its wake a wry humor. "Do you have a shovel handy? The fertilizer's getting pretty high in here.''

"Think about the source of that nickname. The guys were jealous as hell. You were on the fast track to making partner, you weren't interested in them and you were the blonde who made their temperatures rise every time you walked by in your high heels. Hey, of course they were going to try to shoot you down. They had to. To save their self-respect.''

"Men." She shook her head wearily.

"Men," he agreed. "All those caveman genes. Those primitive fight or flight hormones. We're not big on running from challenges, are we?''

The silence built between them. He could hear the tiny slipping sound her blouse made against her skin as she shifted the satchel and its strap caught between her breasts. "Want to know something, Jonas?''

"Sure.''

"If I'd ever had one second's doubt about my decision, all this reminiscing is making me more and more content with the way my life worked out. All that backbiting—I'd forgotten." She sighed, her shoulders slumping as she exhaled. She looked defeated suddenly. Tired. "Games. All that energy spent on such petty stuff. On keeping score. And none of it meant anything. Winning was everything. Nothing else mattered.''

The elevator doors opened, and he backed against one, keeping the entrance open after she entered.

"That's why I sold my share of the firm, Jess. After the Chapman case. You remember the Chapman trial, don't you? And the night the verdict came in?" He wondered if she'd at last admit she remembered that April night she'd spent wrapped up in his arms, he in hers, both of them keeping their demons at bay while the scent of orange blossoms drifted in through the open windows of his apartment and spring-sweet air slid over their bodies.

She leaned her head back against the elevator wall. Shutting her eyes, she said, "You win.''

"This isn't about winning, Jess. I just wanted to know if you'd forgotten.''

"No, Jonas, of course I haven't. And, yes, this is still about winning, about proving your point, your case, about wearing your opponent down, trapping him into an admission. Okay. I remember." Opening her eyes, she studied him wearily. "Are we even now? Is the score between us even? Oh, wait,

I forgot. Even isn't good enough, is it? All right, Jonas, I've admitted it. I remember that night. Every second of it. Does that satisfy you?''

''*Satisfy* is a dangerous word, Jess, under the circumstances, don't you think?'' Stroking his hands over her, he'd learned the texture of her skin, of her face that night, a sensory memory that even now, thinking of the feel of her under him, sent the blood pooling to his groin.

''Jonas, please, I'm exhausted. You are, too. What's dangerous here is dredging up old memories. That night was a mistake. For both of us. I pretended I didn't remember because I wanted to salvage whatever pride I could. Can't we close the book on what happened six years ago? On the past?''

''You'd left the firm, Jess, when I came back after my leave of absence. Nobody knew where you'd gone.''

''Really?'' Her head fell back again, and the line of her throat caught the light, gleaming against the shiny pink collar of her blouse, the tiny freckle fading in the light.

''I tried to find you.'' He'd spent money, hours, searching for her. And then, when he couldn't find her, he'd purged the night and the day that preceded it from his memories. They were too closely intertwined, and he didn't want to be reminded at every turn of the verdict he'd won for his client. ''Here's a truth for you, Jess. I was glad when I couldn't find you. I was ashamed of myself. Of what I'd done to you. Of what I'd done in court. When I couldn't find you, I was relieved because I wanted to forget that day, Jess, more than anything I could think of.''

She didn't move.

''But every now and then I'd see a woman who walked like you, who held her head in that arrogant, don't-mess-with-me way you have, and I'd turn and follow her for a block or two. I wanted to explain, to apologize, to make amends.''

''For what?'' Her question was a thread of sound under the *slap-slap* thump of the door against his back. A tiny hatchmark of lines showed on the delicate skin under her closed eyes, and he wanted to brush away the care, the years that had traced them there. ''Why did you think you owed me an apology?''

"It was your first time, Jess."

"Yes," she whispered, eyes shut, lashes fluttering to the rhythm of the blood beating in the thin blue veins that showed in the fragile skin. "It was."

"And I walked away the next morning and left you alone, sleeping. I didn't leave a note. I didn't call."

"No, you didn't." She lifted her shoulders. "I didn't expect you to. Why would I have? I knew what I was doing, Jonas. We—comforted each other that night, if you want to use that word, whatever it means. Sex as comfort, as anodyne. That's what it was, right?" Her voice was so level that Buck wondered what she was hiding from him even now. "I never expected anything more from you. What was done, was done. Over."

"But I didn't take it lightly, either, Jess. You saved me that night."

Her eyelids blinked open. "Did I? That's funny."

"Funny?" He was taken aback. She'd startled him. "What do you—"

She leaned forward and pushed the button for the ground floor. "Jonas, either step away from the doors, or I'm walking down."

"Of course." Stepping off the elevator, he blocked the closing of the door with his foot. "One more point since we're acting as each other's mirror today, Jess. Another similarity we share is that we get real touchy when the emotions get up close and personal. We like playing our lawyer games because it gives us the edge, the control. You and I, Jess, we really like being in control of a situation, don't we? We like having the upper hand, not being at that disadvantage I mentioned earlier."

"Yes, I like knowing what's coming at me around the corner. I don't like surprises." She moved to the side of the elevator. "Goodbye, Jonas. Thank you for all the insights and analysis. Our—conversation has been almost as good as a therapy session. Should I send you a check, along with the new shirt?"

He removed his foot and the doors began to close, shutting

out his view of her. Just before the rubber edges bumped together, he called, "Be seeing you, Jess. I'll come by and collect the shirt."

The doors shut and green numbers flashed slowly on the display overhead until the car reached the third floor.

No sooner had the doors closed than the old chill settled around his shoulders, moved into his bones. In all the humming, clicking, noisiness of the hospital, he was alone, and he found he missed Jessie, missed her combination of vinegar and honey. Missed the way she kept him from sinking back into the funk he'd been in for months now. She kept him on his toes, and he felt more alive than he'd felt in ages.

Staring at the unmoving green light, he realized he didn't have to let her go.

He could make up for the way he'd treated her six years ago.

The numbers began flashing. *Two.* Standing watching the numbers mark the floors, he realized that he needed to make that kind of gesture, to right the wrong he'd done her.

In some way, he owed her. Paying that old debt would erase some of his self-revulsion about that period in his life. And if he settled that psychic debt, would it matter that he would be cleansing his own soul at the same time?

Shoving open the exit door, he leaped down the stairwell, three and four steps at a time, racing against the ancient elevator's leisurely drop.

When he reached the hospital lobby, he popped through the fire door in time once more to see her disappear around a corner toward the automatic front doors. Breaking into a run, he took off after her, following the glimmer of no-color fabric and streaky blond braid into the parking lot.

As his boots pounded against the hot pavement, he felt as if he'd plunged inside his dream, searching desperately for something just out of sight, something just around the corner that eluded his grasp, his understanding, and left him with outstretched, empty hands and an aching heart.

Chapter Seven

Scraping glue and mayonnaise off her fingers, Jessica surveyed her kingdom with satisfaction.

Worn-out by moving and trying to keep Gopher, the house and her job all on track, she'd taken one of her vacation days. She needed time to organize the stuff of their lives. Too many boxes were still unpacked, too many half-completed projects were piling up. Four weeks of living out of suitcases and boxes was enough. For her peace of mind, she needed to get her house in some kind of order. This morning she and Gopher had peeled cabbage rose wallpaper off his bedroom walls and washed them down. Her plan for the afternoon was to slap a couple of coats of glossy white paint on his room and call it decorated.

That would be one complete project, reason for applause and celebration, reason for squandering a vacation day on work. Contented, she rolled her shoulders, easing the kinks out. She'd enjoyed the day with her son.

And, if she were completely honest with herself, she wasn't eager to run into Jonas at the hospital, not after the fool she'd made of herself the day before. She hadn't cried in years. She knew better than to cry about the patients she worked with.

They needed her skills, not her tears. Yesterday, though, she'd made a mistake. Several of them, actually. She rubbed the pinhead-size pieces of wallpaper glue between her fingers, letting the pieces sift to the floor.

She'd needed today.

She'd needed this time to remind herself of why she'd made the choices she had, to regain her equilibrium. To remember that she was Jessie McDonald, mother, therapist, homeowner.

Stretching her paste-flecked legs in front of her, she looked up at the old porch ceiling with its flaking paint high overhead. Today, even that evidence of more projects couldn't spoil the lovely contentment lapping through her.

The ceiling fan circled slowly, stirring the air. Under the high-roofed shelter of the screened porch, the movement of muggy air against Jessie's skin was almost cool, turning the porch into a shadowy, cool cave. On the glass-topped table beside her at head level, two half-eaten cheese sandwiches hung over the edge of a bright green plate.

Looking up at them through the glass, she pointed to the plate. "Flying saucer at two o'clock, Gopher."

Flat on his back with his feet entangled in the ironworks of the pedestal supporting the glass, Gopher drummed his feet. Putting a paper straw to his mouth, he blew a paper pellet up at the table and the plate. The pellet struck the bottom of the plate. Rolling onto his side, he pretended to dodge. "Patooey!" Around him, tiny paper wads littered the floor. "The crumb-bums lose," he crowed.

"Any chance they were friendly and bringing world peace?" She pulled open the bag of pop-on mouths, ears, hats, noses and accessory parts for the spud-shaped toy in front of her.

"Nah." Gopher rolled another paper pellet. "They were going to blow up the world, that's what. Crumb-bums do that, Mommy," he added earnestly. "Every time. Boom." For emphasis, he bounced his rump against the floor. "And that's that. But I won 'em this time!" he tacked on, his chipmunk face smiling with satisfaction. "Gopher did it again! I saved the whole wide world!"

Men, Jessie thought again. Somebody always had to win. To lose. Had to be the way their brains were wired. Or the effect of all that testosterone sloshing through them. "Lucky for you their weapons were a little cheesy," she said wryly.

Rolling his eyes, Gopher aimed his straw at Skeezix, who lay like a washed-out rug on the chaise longue next to the table, tongue hanging out, eyes half-closed.

"Whoa, Captain." She captured his leg. "Nonliving targets only."

The straw trembled. Gopher's inclination to let fly was written all over his face as he looked at her, checking to see if she were serious.

"What if you hurt Skeezix?"

Hearing his name, the dog opened one eye, scratched his nose and rolled over onto his side. Gopher looked at him, back at her. "I won't hurt Skeezes."

"You might."

"I would not be mean to my Skeezes," he crooned. "I *luuuuv* my Skeezes. But what if that's a crumb-bumbian in disguise? Might be." He wrinkled his nose. "He might not be my Skeezes."

"Gopher, think about what I said." Jessie lifted an eyebrow at him and waited. No wonder kids needed two parents. Even one kid could wear a woman out. Would it be easier to be a single dad? Nah. She grinned. Except, maybe, single dads didn't obsess so much about whether destroying the universe of the crumb-bums was instilling antisocial values in an impressionable four-and-a-half-year-old. She leaned over and rumpled his hair. "Gopher?"

The straw lowered, changed angles. A round pellet hit the flowerpot overflowing with geraniums. Round-eyed, he smiled innocently at her. "I destroyed the stronghold."

"So you did, sugar. Come on over and help me finish this creation. What do you think?" She held out a set of eyes, one brown, one blue.

"I don't think so." He took the blue eye, clattered other toy parts helter-skelter in a search for the matching blue one.

While he excavated through flowers and noses, Jessie stuck

wide red lips on the brown plastic head. "There. A vision of loveliness."

"Mommy's silly, silly, silly," Gopher chanted, hooking his short fingers into the corners of his mouth and pulling his lips into a pretzel shape.

"But—" Jessie scrabbled through the assortment of plastic accessories "—where are the glasses and flowers? I saw them a second ago—" She lifted her head. The miniature set of plastic frames adorned the pudgy face beaming at her. "Hmm. Yes, Gopher, a very intellectual look. It suits you. But I think Mrs. P. should definitely be wearing glasses and flowers on her hat." She grabbed another set of round glasses and stuck them onto the figure. Leaning back, she surveyed the lumpy head. "Perfect."

"Nope." Gopher picked up another part and replaced the hat with it. "Now she can ear you." Roaring with laughter, he tumbled around Jessie, his fanny thumping the floor with each somersault. "She can *ear* you, Mommy, she can *ear* you!"

The ear perched like a shallow hat on top of the plastic head. Jessie pushed her glasses back up the bridge of her nose and captured her son. "You're a stinker, that's what you are, George McDonald. Do you 'ear' *me?*" She tickled his belly and then swooped in to blow a raspberry onto his belly as he shrieked at top volume.

"Hello, Jessie. Gopher."

The voice was silky cool in the lunchtime heat, sliding over her like the stroke of a Popsicle. She shivered and looked up.

Confound the man.

Jessie looked through the screening with a resigned expression. "Come in, Jonas." She sat up, pushed her hair back and straightened her T-shirt, tucking it into place.

"Mister!" Gopher jumped up, trying to see around her. "Hey, mister! Want some memonade and samiches?" He held out one of the sandwiches to Jonas. "I only ate part. You kin have the rest," he offered, pushing the bread against the screen.

Jessie scrambled to her feet, pulling down too-short shorts

and the shirt that seemed to have a mind to wander northward to her ribs. "Well, don't just stand there in the sun, Jonas. You look silly baking your brains. Come on inside."

"Sure," Jonas said with an easy smile that sent her heart plummeting right down to her toes. "How could I refuse an offer like that?" He pulled open the screen door that bent, wobbled and finally whacked back into its frame. Looking at it, he frowned. "Door needs leveling, doesn't it?"

"It opens. It shuts." Jessie reached up to tug off the rubber band confining her hair, scooped the weight of it higher and secured it once again with the band. Perspiration dripped down her spine, down between her breasts, and she felt as if she were burning up inside, all the cool laziness of the past half hour evaporating in the amused appreciation of his eyes as they drifted to the dark line of perspiration gluing her shirt to her midline. "What do you want, Jonas, not that you're not welcome, but why were you here?"

"I've come to make you a proposition, Jessie."

"No, thanks."

"Here, mister." Gopher handed him the squashed sandwich and trotted back to the table, climbing up onto a chair and rummaging through paper cups.

Jonas folded the sandwich, tucked it tidily into his mouth and chewed. "Tasty. Thanks, Gopher." Brushing off his hands, he addressed Jessie again. "Don't you want to hear what I have to say?"

Gopher looked their way, giggled and clapped his hands over his face. "Mommy can ear you, mister!" His eyes peeped over the tops of his hands at her. "Can't you?"

Jessie had to give the man credit. He didn't blink, stumble, or say something dumb. Instead, his gaze scanning the porch, he stooped, picked up Mrs. P. and regarded the toy with a serious frown before shooting Jessie a glance that almost had her giggling like her son.

"Ah. Doing major surgery, are we?" He handed Jessie the bespectacled, be-eared head. "Considering a malpractice suit, maybe? I know a good lawyer."

"Hmm. So do I. In a pinch." In spite of herself, Jessie

snickered, then recovered and pulled her features into some semblance of dignity, difficult to do with shorts riding up and the damp spots on her shirt imitating cellophane.

Gopher snorted, tumbled off the chair and righted himself. "Surgery. Yeah." He hefted the pitcher filled with melting ice and lemonade. Pouring it into the cup that had landed with him on the floor, he giggled again. Picking up another plastic piece, he pitched it toward Jonas. "Maybe Mrs. P. nose you, too." Sending Jonas a mischievous grin, he let loose a whoop of laughter. "If she can't ear you!"

Skeezix climbed off the chaise and ambled over to Jonas, tipping up his chin for scratching. *"Urrrff,"* he said by way of greeting.

"The dog likes me, Jess." Jonas scratched along Skeezix's jawbone while the dog shivered in ecstasy.

Jessie knew the feeling. Her own skin rippled in response to that long, lingering stroke of Jonas's lean hand over the dog. The damp spot under her breasts turned icy as Jonas continued petting Skeezix and didn't let his gaze move from her face. Oh, the devil knew what he was doing to her.

With a sweeping pat along Skeezix's back that sent the dog into shuddering adoration, Jonas smiled at her, his face lighting up with sly mischief in much the same way Gopher's had. "Dogs are good judges of character."

Balefully she glared at the hapless dog. "I'm thinking of getting a cat."

Skeezix ignored her.

Jonas sent her a silky smile. "Cats are nice. They like me, too."

"Really? Maybe I should think about getting a fish."

"Fish don't have much personality. Not that I can tell, anyway. They don't tend to cuddle up."

"Good. That suits me fine. A nice big bowl of fish is sounding better by the minute."

"Too bad. Cuddling can be very—neighborly." He scratched Skeezix's ears.

Jessie couldn't decide whether to box Jonas's ears or pretend to ignore him. He'd come knocking on her door with some purpose in mind, and until he was ready to reveal it, he'd try to keep her off balance by flirting, by distracting her, by scratching the damn dog's ears until Jessie herself wanted to wag her tail and whine in ecstasy. She ran her finger under the edge of her suddenly damp neckline and then snapped her fingers. "Skeez! Come!"

He edged closer to Jonas.

Skeezix might be dumb, but he was no fool. He obviously knew a good thing when he found it, and Jessie wasn't about to give him another order to ignore. "Quite a technique you have there, Jonas. But then Skeezix is a sucker for anybody who'll give him the time of day."

"Is he?" Jonas's long fingers trailed languorously down the bumps of Skeezix's spine. "Good dog."

The good dog collapsed in an adoring, ignominious heap on Jonas's shoes. Jessie rolled her eyes and gave up.

Gopher, his tongue caught between his teeth, carried a dripping cup of lemonade toward Jonas, stumbled, caught himself and continued, lemonade sloshing with each careful step. "Here, mister." He handed Jonas the dented, quarter-full cup.

Jonas saluted him. "Thanks. This will hit the spot."

"What spot?" One foot on top of the other, Gopher waited.

With his free hand, Jonas patted his stomach. "This spot."

"Oh. Okay." Frowning, Gopher scanned Jonas. Finally, putting his hands in the vicinity of his hips, Gopher quizzed him. "Where's your cowboy clothes? How come you're dressed silly today? And where's your hat? I like your hat. And your boots. You got on reg'lar shoes," he finished in an accusing tone. "You're not my Sir Cowboy."

For the first time since she'd heard his voice, Jessie noticed Jonas's clothes. "Yes, Jonas, I almost didn't recognize you without your outfit. Tan chinos? Mushroom brown shirt?" The creamy browns made her lust for a mocha latte. Badly. She fanned her face. "You went shopping?"

"In T.J.'s closet." He shrugged, and the movement of his shoulders under the cotton tightened the fabric across the slope of his shoulders dangerously. The slacks barely avoided being flood pants, but the effect was elegantly casual, cool.

Hadn't he packed a bag? Had he really gone tube-city with his investments and been reduced to secondhand clothing? She couldn't imagine what might have brought Jonas to such a point. Dismay stirred in her. "You're wearing your brother's clothes?"

"Sure. They fit." Bare ankles gleamed as he crossed one foot over the other and struck a mock-model pose. Holding the paper cup carefully, he drank from it, the freshly shaved hollows of his cheeks and chin drawing her gaze. "Don't you think so?"

Oh, she knew what she thought. She missed the dusty cowboy with his beard-shadowed face and his comfortable seediness, especially in her current disheveled state with Gopher's lemonade-sticky hand joining the smear of dirt along her thigh. "I think you look very nice, Jonas, and I'm still wondering why you're here."

"A couple of things. I brought Gopher the toy you left behind at the grocery store." Sticking a hand into the close-fitting pocket of his borrowed pants, he retrieved a metallic-painted, candy apple red car. "Here." He held the car out to Gopher.

"For me?" Gopher stepped forward, one hand out, one still stuck against her leg. "Boyohboyohboy," he whispered, turning the shrink-wrapped box over and over. "Red! I *luuuuv red*," he said, poking at the plastic.

Jessie's fingers curled against her leg. Jonas must have bought the car the night she'd run into him at the Palmetto Mart. The car had been the last red one on the shelf. She'd checked. "Why?"

He knew what she meant. "Because?" A dull flush touched the jut of his cheekbones.

"Not good enough." She felt as though something were cracking inside her. Not even knowing for whom she was buying the car, Jonas had seen her leave the car behind and had bought it, planning, even after that brief encounter, on seeing her again.

"I don't know why I bought it, Jess. I just did. You seemed

so reluctant to leave it behind and, what the hell, I bought it."
He thumped the edge of the door with the back of his hand.

"You shouldn't have."

"Well, I did. It's a done deal, okay? And I'm not going to
rip it out of Gopher's hands and return it. Besides," he said,
tipping his head toward her son, "I don't think it's
returnable."

Gopher had crumpled the plastic, flattened the thin cardboard, and pulled out the miniature car. "I'm gonna drive my
very fast car," he said, looking at her. "Outside? On my
track?"

"Sure."

"C'mon, Skeezes!" Gopher smacked open the screen door,
leaped off the top wooden step and caromed off the handrail,
heading for the sandbox with Skeezix wandering sluggishly
behind him. The door wobbled on its hinges and Jonas caught
the handle, pulling the door shut. *"Vroom!"* Gopher dived
belly first into the sandbox, the car in front of him. *"Vroom,
vroom!"*

"Oh, Jonas."

"Oh, Jessie," he mocked, but his smile turned the turbulent
blue of his eyes to the shade of the Gulf under a hot sun, that
clear, welcoming blue that invited, tempted, lured you into its
depths. "It's just a three-dollar toy. No big deal."

Jessie tried to breathe past the aching awareness deep inside
her. That night in the store he hadn't recognized her. He'd
acted on instinct, that same instinct that had sent them into
each other's arms on a spring night long ago, a night she'd
tried to forget and never had, a night that had changed her life
in ways she never wanted him to know.

Jonas could talk all he wanted to about the games they
played, the way each tried to maintain the balance of power
between them, and he was right, but he'd never understand
how important that balance was to her, now, more than ever.

Because he'd always held the upper hand and never known
it.

She hoped he never found out the ultimate power he unwittingly held over her, a power he'd never sought, never wanted.

Then, when she was least prepared, he sandbagged her. "So, you going to let me tell you about my proposition?"

Jessie took a deep breath and tried to collect her scattered thoughts, tried to forget the way Gopher's face had glowed when Jonas had handed him the car. "Any reason why I'd want to?"

"Might be to your advantage." He strolled over to the table and stood there, his back to her.

Wishing he'd turn around so that she could see his face, Jessie muttered, "I doubt that."

His shoulders moved, the muscles flexing beneath the creamy shirt fabric as he stacked paper cups and plates on top of each other. "I need a room, Jess." One shoulder lifted in a barely perceptible movement that pulled the shirt tight against the side of his rib cage, shaping the ridged muscles underneath and tempting her to smooth her hand across them. "I'd like to rent a room from you."

Her throat went dry. "What?"

"I'd like to stay here for a few days. If you'll let me."

"Impossible." Her hands fluttered at her throat and she forced them into the pockets of her cutoffs. Her finger slid through the hole in the right pocket and against the skin of her thigh. "I can't imagine—"

He turned, braced his hands in back of him on the table. "A swap, Jess. That's what I'm suggesting."

"Jonas, I'm not following you at all." She refused to sit even though her knees were shaking. She couldn't think, couldn't begin to guess what he had in mind. And, as certain as the rain in summer, Jonas would have another motive behind the one up-front. He always did.

Not always, the faint voice in her head buzzed. *Once he didn't. Once he was very straightforward, intent on nothing except her, touching her, kissing her, stroking her until her skin burned, melted, fused with his.*

Under her forefinger, the skin of her thigh went icy hot, and she yanked her hand out of her pocket. "Better spell out what you mean, Jonas. It's been a while since I've wandered down the highways and byways of a mind like yours and, quite frankly, you're a couple of miles ahead of me today."

"It's simple. I need a place to stay. I'm hoping you and I can work out some kind of mutually agreeable arrangement."

"What? You want to stay here? In my house?" Her whole body buzzed now, that sly little voice vibrating through her from head to toe, and all she could think of was that night years ago, that night when she'd learned about her body, her *self*. To have Jonas in her home? Within sight? Where every time she looked up she'd see him? Inhale the scent of him? Even her lips buzzed with memory.

As he turned his head, looking away from her, out toward her son, a shadow passed over the sun, over his face, hiding his eyes from her. "You look like you have a lot of work here and could use a helping hand. I'm offering to swap sweat equity and cash if you'll let me stay here for a week. Or so."

"Why?"

"Daddy's going to be staying a bit longer in the hospital. I want to be near him."

"Why can't you stay where you are now? Aren't you at your brother's ranch?"

"No." He turned around to face her. "I'm bunking for the moment at Maxie's Tropical Motel. You remember Maxie, don't you?"

She did. Tall, earthy, Maxie Sweeney had been a client of Jack Keane's. "Yes." Jessie knew the motel, too. Clean. Cheap. A shade this side of tacky. Sterile. Not a place to be by yourself. "Can't you move out with the rest of your family, then, at T.J.'s?"

"No."

Jessie frowned. In his clipped response was the unspoken truth she'd seen yesterday in his father's hospital room. No matter how much his family loved him, Jonas saw himself as separate, not quite one of them. "But—"

"Anyway, there isn't room. Not with everyone camping out there. Mama, Jilly and Hank and their kids. And, of course, T.J. and Callie and Charlie. Nine people. It's a crowd."

"But one more person?" She almost blurted out the real question on her mind: *Why do you want to stay here?* "That doesn't seem so impossible, does it?"

"I'd be in the way." His face turned stubborn. "What do you think, Jess? Can you see a way to make room for me here? An arrangement that would be fair to you?"

"Jonas, I can't—" She stopped.

"Think about it, will you?" He gestured toward the yard, the ceiling, the paint spatters on her legs. "You could use an extra pair of hands, couldn't you, Jess?"

Whatever was going on inside him, Jessie could see that staying at the ranch with his family would be an ordeal. He could afford to stay at Maxie's. Couldn't he? She frowned. What did she know about the state of his finances? Had he gone broke financing and working his own ranch? What did she know about anything that had happened to him in the past five years? Maybe he couldn't afford Maxie's.

Still, it wasn't her problem. She rubbed at the dirt spot on her cutoffs and phrased her refusal. "Look, Jonas, I'm sorry, but there must be somewhere else—"

"What's the problem, Jess? I'm a very handy man to have around the house."

Exactly, she thought. Too handy. She risked a glance at his clever hands resting casually on the table. Oh, no, she'd be crazy—

"Those steps are about to collapse with mildew and termite rot."

"I'll call the exterminator. The carpenter." She backed up before she realized what she was doing as he stepped nearer, the ceiling fan ruffling a strand of his dark red-gold hair.

"Expensive."

"I can afford them."

"Can you?" He surveyed the crumbling posts supporting the sagging screen, let his eyes roam over the floor planks that badly needed repairing and staining. "Lot of work here, Jess. Expenses could add up real fast."

"I took out a big mortgage. To cover extras like repairs."

She folded her arms. "I'm not broke. I can provide what Gopher and I need."

"I'm not surprised. You never liked asking for help." He picked at the wood of one of the columns and sawdust drifted thickly to the floor. "Big mortgage, huh?"

She nodded even though she suspected he was laughing at her, that something in her face amused him. "Very big mortgage. But the house is mine. All mine. And I can make the payments."

"Congratulations." He dusted his hands. "But, with a very big mortgage, you might find you'd like to save a dollar here and there. I work cheap, Jess. Just a room. A little space. That's all I'm asking."

What she wanted to say was that she couldn't afford him, his price had always been too high for her, but that admission wasn't possible, had never been possible and, anyway, he was moving right into her space, walking her backward until her fanny bumped the edge of the rotting wood railing. And then he lifted his thumb, brushing the corner of her mouth, turning her into liquid sunshine.

"Mayonnaise." He showed her the white smear on his thumb, and then he grinned. "Or are you so ticked off with me that you're starting to foam at the mouth?"

Laughter bubbled inside her, slow and easy, a rich welling up of amusement. "Could be. I haven't had my rabies shot."

"Ah, a dangerous woman."

A dangerous man, that's what Jonas was.

His bare ankle slid against her leg and she shivered. His eyes smiled back at her, inviting her to laugh at him, at herself, to join him in the lazy intimacy of the moment. He rested his forearms lightly, so lightly, on her shoulders, and yet she felt their weight, welcomed it, welcomed the warmth of his touch against her hot skin. Stooping, he brought his face close to hers, his breath mingling with hers, making her ache inside with old hungers and longings.

"Can't you see your way clear to letting me stay, Jess?" His eyes met hers, and deep down inside where she'd bet a year's salary he didn't know anything showed, she saw the loneliness, the need.

Her house.

And Jonas in it. With her. With Gopher.

"Please?"

Such a simple request. Such an impossible request from him to her. She could refuse him. She knew she could. But she couldn't look away from his gaze, all that bright blue brilliance and deep in its depths a soul-deep bleakness calling to her. "Jonas—" She started to shake her head regretfully, to tell him once and for all that she couldn't give him what he wanted.

His forehead bumped hers, or maybe she only imagined the skim of his nose against hers, the weight of his mouth over hers.

And then he stepped back, putting space between them, and yet in the air stirring between them she still felt his touch, the weight of his hands, his mouth on her.

"Well, can't blame a fellow for trying."

He smiled, the smile sliding off his face, and his eyes were empty, lost, she thought, but, really, his finances weren't her problem. Nor was his relationship with his family. She couldn't help him. She'd had enough trouble saving herself, carving out a life for her and Gopher, and why oh why was she risking everything she'd worked for and telling Jonas, "All right, Jonas. For a week. Or less."

"You won't be sorry, Jess." Relief flickered in the brief smile he sent her.

"Oh, I'm sure I will be. Sooner or later." She glared at him, annoyed with herself, worried about him in spite of all the reasons not to be, and dismayed by what she'd let herself in for.

"I won't get in your way."

"Really?" She rested her hands on the railing, her knees trembling with the effort not to reach up and grab the collar points of that damn coffee-colored shirt and tug him forward, taste the breath that had merged with hers. Her fingers dug into the railing. "You think you can stay out of my way, Jonas? Is that what you're promising?"

"Scout's honor." He crossed his heart with a flick of his fingers.

"Were you ever actually a Boy Scout, Jonas?"

He just stood there, smiling.

"I didn't think so," she said crossly, moving to the side to pass him.

He caught her arm. His palm was warm and rough against the skin of her inner arm. Her stomach tensed, loosened, and her nipples tightened. Defensive, she lifted her chin, ready to shoot him down in flames, to take back her reluctant offer.

And then, with three words, he disarmed her. "Jess, thank you."

He was already in her way, in her space, crowding her with nothing more than his sheer overwhelming physical presence. As for not crowding her emotionally? Intellectually? Not likely unless the world had suddenly reversed its poles.

Staring into his eyes, watching the way he focused intently on her while keeping his innermost thoughts to himself, Jessie knew she'd caught a tiger by the tail and she had no one to blame but herself. Like the first time she'd let him into her life, let him past her guard, she'd fooled herself into thinking she knew what she was doing.

And she never had.

Not where Jonas was concerned.

Hours later, paint cans opened and emptied around them, Buck laid the paint roller in the tray and wiped his hands down a pair of T.J.'s oldest jeans. "So, Jess, isn't this better than climbing up and down a ladder?"

"You've finished the ceiling already?" Her tongue caught between her teeth in concentration, she was painting around the edge of the window on the far side of Gopher's room. She lifted the narrow brush and faced him. Paint splattered her hair, her glasses, her nose. He reckoned she didn't know she'd sat in a puddle of paint and left a charming bull's-eye right on one round cheek. "That was fast."

"Me too, me too!" Gopher poked his head out of the closet. Paint plopped on his sneakers in big fat drops. "I'm fast like Mr. Jonas."

Buck was glad the kid had finally settled on a name. "Sir Cowboy" had seemed a shade formal. Under the circumstances.

"Me and you are a good team," Gopher said, leaning comfortably against Buck's leg, a trail of paint marking his progress from the closet to Buck's side. Like his mother, the kid seemed to have taken a bath in the shiny paint. His hair stuck up in stiff, white points where he'd leaned against the wall or patted it with his hands. "I *luuv* painting my room. I want to paint stars on my ceiling now."

"No stars on the ceiling," Jessie said. "But we can hang some from the windows."

"Or in the closet where it's dark."

"We'll see."

Gopher looked up at Buck and yawned. "Stars are nice, huh, Mr. Jonas?" Paint ran down his arm and on to Buck's shoes. "I should have stars in my closet, huh?"

Buck wasn't going to touch that question with a fifteen-foot pole. He knew what the squirt was doing, but he kind of hoped the kid got away with it. "Why do you want stars, Gopher?"

The kid looked up at him with the most amazed glance, as if the answer were obvious. "To shine, of course." His face squinched up, and Buck figured only good manners kept Gopher from rolling his eyes in disbelief.

"Well, of course. Reckon I should have figured that out for myself, huh?"

"I reckon you should." Gopher turned him loose and wandered across the plastic drop cloth to the paint tray and dropped his brush onto it. "Now I'm going to make my handprint in my closet because I always do wherever I live." He smiled winningly at Buck. "You make one, too."

"Uh, maybe your mama—" Buck checked Jessie's reaction.

"Go ahead." Her voice teased him with its weary huskiness. Her shoulders sagged with exhaustion, and blue tinged the skin under her eyes. "Closets are for storing memories. We do handprints, height checks. Gopher and I like our closets." She sighed and looked blankly at the brush still in her hand. "I need to finish this window and then let's call it a day."

"You were planning to do this whole room today? By yourself?"

"I help, too. You forgotted me." Gopher spoke before Jessie could answer.

"Yeah, kid, I guess I did."

"I did the closet. All alone."

"Well, let's check it out." Buck squatted next to the paint tray. "Here, give me your hand. If we're going to do a print, I think we should make it the best one anyone ever saw." Rolling Gopher's small, dimpled hand into the paint, Buck added, "Got any markers?"

Gopher's eyes went doughnut round. "I don't write on *any* walls with markers. I am *very* responsible."

Jessie stood in front of him, her hands on her hips. With the paintbrush-wielding hand, she tucked back a loop of curl that had worked its way free of her braid. "What did you have in mind, Jonas?"

He looked up at her, past the nicely rounded length of tanned legs and curving thighs, past the swooping indentation of waist and hip. His gaze lingered on the tissue-thin cotton of her T-shirt where paint stuck it to her abdomen and to her breasts. As he watched, she inhaled. Cotton tightened over the slopes of her breasts and clung to small pointed nipples. Leaning back on his heels, he said, "You want to know what I have in mind, Jess?" And then, unable to resist, he looked straight into her eyes and smiled.

She blushed, not a delicate, pallid pink, but a deep, vivid red, the color flashing up the slender column of her neck and staining her face. "With the markers, Jonas," she said in a strangled voice.

"Why, darlin', nothing more excitin' than adding a little color to Gopher's closet. Disappointed?"

"Impossible man," she muttered, turning on her heel and

stalking out of the room, her paintbrush clutched in one narrow fist.

"Mommy's not mad," Gopher said reassuringly, patting Buck's knee. "Don't worry. When she's mad, she says so. But I do not think we should use markers."

"You don't, huh?" Buck studied the kid's wide blue eyes. Funny how kids all kind of looked alike. Gopher reminded him of his cousin Sarah's Nicholas, of T.J.'s Charlie.

"Nope. Absolutely nope." Gopher shook his head over and over.

Buck stood up, taking the kid's paint-free hand in his. Holding Jessie's son's hand in his, the small, trusting grip fastened on to him, Buck envied his brothers more than he ever had before.

And when he and Gopher had finished plastering their handprints side by side in the closet, a "memory" as Gopher called it, Buck dated and signed the prints, the small one touchingly vulnerable next to the man-size outline.

"Me and you. Forever," Gopher said, looking at the prints and yawning.

Buck didn't answer. There was no forever for him with this kid who wasn't his, but who, if circumstances had been different, if he'd been a different kind of man, if Jess—

If.

But Gopher was some other man's child.

Not his.

But he could have been.

Chapter Eight

"G'night, Mr. Jonas." A gray-blue blanket hung from Gopher's fist. He lifted his other hand to Buck.

"He wants to give you a hug. I think." Jessie lifted an eyebrow and crossed her arms. Her wet hair hung in long curly strips down her back, rivulets of water dripping onto the shrieking pink shirt that hit her midcalf.

She and Gopher were bathed and ready for bed. The scent of soap and fabric softener lingered in the air, a cozy, domestic smell, seductive.

He wanted to stay with them. He didn't want to leave this nighttime cocoon. He wanted to stay in Jessie's house with her and her son. The middle of summer and he felt as if he were walking out of a safe place into dead winter.

He blinked. He couldn't remember the last time he'd wanted to stay anywhere, but during the long hours of the afternoon and early evening, Jessie and her son had entangled him in their routine. They'd made a place for him in their teasing, at their table, making him scramble the "kitchen sink" omelets and treating him as casually as Skeezix.

He'd felt in those hours as though he'd come home.

Maybe it was the way Gopher tagged along behind him, as

if the goofy kid had decided Buck was his. With the uncritical acceptance of a four-year-old, Gopher had claimed him.

Maybe it was that damn Skeezix, who couldn't seem to refrain from drooling all over T.J.'s pants and shoes. T.J. was going to get a new wardrobe out of this adventure, that was for sure.

Or maybe it was Jessie and the way her eyes kept following him, and the exasperated way she drew her eyebrows together every time she caught herself looking at him.

He'd provoked those sideways glances. He liked those unconscious responses, liked getting a rise out of her. He enjoyed knowing he could sneak behind her cool, stand-clear attitude. Most of all, he'd grown addicted to that snap of electricity between them.

The tug of a hand on his slacks brought him out of his drifting thoughts. "I'm waiting right here." Gopher yawned.

Jessie yawned in sympathy, and Buck found his own jaws stretching in concert with them.

"No sneak attacks, Gopher?" Buck stooped down. His knees bumped Gopher's leg.

"Nope." His round face was bath-rosy and steamy-wet. "G'bye." A wet kiss landed on Buck's cheek and a chubby arm wrapped around his neck. "I liked painting with you. See you tomorrow."

"Yeah. Reckon you will." Buck stood up and watched Gopher's rump vanish toward the stairs, the blanket dragging along the floor and Skeezix ambling after him.

"I hope the night goes well for Hoyt. For you." Arms crossed, bare feet naked of polish, she faced him. Then, sighing, she held out a shiny new key. "You'll need this in the morning."

He took the key from her. Her fingers were pruney from her bath, and the key was warm from her grip. "All right. Thanks." He would be coming back here. Coming—

Home. He blinked.

"Jonas?" Jessie frowned at him. "Are you all right?"

"Yeah." He tossed the key up and down. He'd thought he could do her a favor by working around her house. He'd thought he could repay an old debt by spending a few hours he'd never miss pounding nails and painting walls in her house. But she'd turned the tables on him, it seemed, because he wanted to come back to her. To her son. To Jessie's house with its rooms needing paint and the porch with its sagging steps and falling-down posts. To Jessie's kitchen where the pipes rattled and leaked.

"Sure?" Without her glasses, her blue eyes were soft and unfocused, sleepy bedroom eyes that lured him closer.

He took a step. Stopped. "I'm fine. Just thinking about some things."

"Your dad?" Tenderness softened her posture, loosened the lines of her body as she leaned toward him, her face concerned. "Call. If you want to."

"Thanks." Buck tucked the key in his pocket and turned away. The effort it took to leave her, to leave this house, astonished him. Looked like the joke was on him after all. "I won't wake you."

"Believe me, you will." Her laugh was rueful. "I don't think I've had a good night's sleep for four and a half years."

Buck looked up the stairs. "He's a wanderer, huh?"

"How about finding him in the front yard during a rainstorm one night?"

"I can see why you have all the locks. I thought you were just being security conscious."

"I am." She shrugged. "But instead of keeping people out, I need to keep my son in. Gopher has absolutely no fear."

"That's good." Buck had been that way himself. He'd woken up one night when he was ten and taken the car out for a drive, returned it and the keys and no one had ever known. Well, maybe T.J. had had his suspicions, but he'd never said anything, not even to Buck, so maybe T.J. had been oblivious, too. Now, looking at the soft lines of anxiety in Jessie's forehead, Buck added, "That's bad, I guess?"

"If you're the parent, you bet. If you're the kid, it's a hoot. Some days I wish I were the kid." Her eyebrow did that little dance step up and back down. "You'd better go, Jonas."

"I reckon." He liked the way her mouth pursed over the *J*

in his name, the soft sibilance as she drew out the last syllable. "Thanks, Jess, for letting me stay here."

"Well, shoot. *Maxie's*. You couldn't stay there. I mean, Maxie's terrific, but—"

"It would have been lonely." He fingered the key in his pocket, tracing its jagged edges and curves. Without asking, she'd handed over her key. Prickly, edgy, keep-your-distance Jessie McDonald had given him the key to her house without a second thought.

"You don't have to worry about being lonely here." Her mouth curved up in amusement. "Too much happens. Sometimes I think a ringmaster would help. This week I've had the plumber, the electrician, Lolly. Actually the electrician and I are thinking of running off together. I think it would be cheaper in the long run." She tugged the neck of her shirt, wound the man's tie she'd used to belt it around her palm. "Well, you must want to leave, and I'm keeping you here. It's your fault if I am, Jonas. Those impeccable manners of yours would keep you standing here for hours." Her shrug was self-conscious, and he wondered what she was thinking.

"It's not manners keeping me standing here, Jess."

The tie slipped through her fingers. "Jonas, I can't go to bed with you. Not again. I have a child and my life is—" Embarrassment colored her face as she studied her toes.

"I know, Jess."

"I'm sorry," she whispered.

"Because you can't make love with me?" He took one enormous step and lifted the wet mass of her hair in one hand, sliding the other underneath, up close against the tender back of her neck. "Or because you were blunt?"

"Yes." She nodded.

"Okay. Both. I understand."

"I had to say something. All this—" She waved her hand and it bumped his chin.

"All this tension and history and stuff between us. Even after five, five and a half years, the sparks are there, right?" He threaded his fingers through the damp strands of her hair, spreading them across her shoulders.

She nodded again and he rested his chin on top of her head, breathing in the flower-scented dampness. "I had to make sure you understood, that you didn't expect—" Her shoulders lifted and his arms slipped over the rounded corners, down her side, rested on the slight swell of her hips.

"You didn't want any misunderstandings."

"Exactly." Her shaky sigh of relief trembled against him. "I knew you'd understand."

He did. She was warning him off, setting up the boundaries, making sure once more that all the cards were on the table. So why did he have the sense that she was hiding something? Like a magician saying "look here" in order to keep the audience from seeing the sleight of hand? Or maybe he was tired and imagining undertones where there weren't any, but he needed some clarification of his own. "Jess, why did you make love with me that night? I always wondered. It was— out of character."

She went very still. Finally she lifted her head and met his searching gaze. "Because I wanted to."

"Nothing more?" He didn't know what he was fishing for, but he still couldn't reconcile the action with what he knew about her.

"Nothing more." She shook her head and droplets of water dotted his shirt, his face. "You came back into the office and I was working late. You were in a strange mood, a surprising one since you'd won the case for your client, and—" She touched one of the damp spots on his chest. "And we made love. You wanted to, I wanted to. We were both adults. Nothing more." She smoothed her finger over the spot again, and her touch curled his stomach into knots. "Go on to the hospital, Jonas. You don't owe me anything."

He jerked back, captured her wrists as she started to move away. "What do you mean?"

"Oh, I know you and your finely tuned sense of responsibility. Good heavens, you turned yourself inside out over a kiss the other day." Her smile was artificial, setting off his alarm. "I only wanted you to understand that what occurred once, wouldn't again, and that you didn't bear any more responsibility for that night than I did. I mean, if that's why you've been working like a maniac all afternoon on my house, you don't have to, hear?" She made a small fist and whacked him gently on the chest.

"Aw, Jess, you figured I was trying to pay you back for that night?" He was, but he hadn't expected her to catch on.

"Yes, Jonas. That thought occurred three or four times to me. Especially after you insisted on working after supper. Not that you're a lazy man, but don't you think that was carrying the work ethic a little far?" She smiled gently and touched his chin. "I'm okay, Jonas. My life is wonderful. I made love with you because—because I wanted to, and I don't regret that night. Now, if you don't mind, I'd like to conclude this discussion." She backed away from him, headed for the stairs. "My son's in my bedroom waiting for his story, Jonas. Good night."

He should have realized she'd see through his clumsy attempt to help her out. Jessie examined a situation the way a diamond jeweler checked a stone's facets, turning it this way, that. He stayed behind, staring after her, watching the light touch her calf muscles as she walked upstairs, the bright pink hem of her shirt—or dress or whatever the hell she wanted to call the thing—tighten and bunch around her hips and rear. "Jess?"

She paused at the landing, her hand on the newel post. "Yes, Jonas? What is it?"

"Why did you want to?"

"Want to what, Jonas?"

"You know."

In the dim light of the upstairs hall, he couldn't be sure whether or not the movement of her mouth was a smile or a whispered comment. The pink shirt glowed, shimmered, and then she turned and disappeared down the hall. He heard her murmured comment to Gopher, and then she shut the door behind her.

All around him her scent mingled with the tang of paint smells, and the boxes and stacks of Jessie's belongings surrounded him, tempting him to stay. He knew she'd be up until midnight unpacking. He wanted to be there with her in those quiet hours. And he wanted to be at the hospital.

Well, he could come back. He had the key to Jessie's house. He turned it over and over in his pocket. He could return.

The next morning, Buck felt two pudgy fingers poking at his eyelids. "Hey, mister, you awake?"

Buck opened one eye. "Nope."

"Sure you are. I can see your eyeball." The bed shook as Gopher leaped off. "Mommy! Mr. Jonas is awake. I bet he's gonna shave, and I'm gonna shave with him."

Buck tried to see the clock radio on the bed stand, but his eyes wouldn't focus on the red numbers. When he'd tiptoed in at five in the morning, Jessie had called out sleepily to him and he'd walked to the door of her bedroom, staring in at her and her son, the two of them shapeless lumps under the cover.

"Jonas," she said on a yawn, "the towels are under the sink in the bathroom. Soap and shampoo are somewhere. You'll find them." The bedsprings creaked as she turned over, sliding her arm around Gopher and drawing him to her. "How's Hoyt?"

"We'll talk in the morning," Buck had said.

He'd stayed at the doorway to her room for a long time, watching her and Gopher as dawn turned the gray light gold. Being in Jessie's house calmed the restless, displaced feelings that had roiled through him for so long. He didn't understand why, but her house eased the loneliness inside him.

And then he'd slipped between the cool sheets on the narrow guest bed and fallen asleep.

The bed bounced again, and Gopher's face peered at him. "When you gonna shave?"

"Mrrghh." His mouth felt like cotton.

"Huh?" Two childish fingers stretched his eyelids open.

"When I can get my brain to communicate with my feet." Was this what Jessie had to deal with every morning? This high-voltage human being who was armed and ready at God only knew what hour? He tried to turn over, but the sheet was caught on something, something that breathed heavily and wetly.

Buck opened his eyes again and met Skeezix's deep brown ones. The sheet underneath the dog's head was damp with dog tongue.

"Gopher! Skeezix! Out!"

"Oh, good. Rescue. Where were you ten minutes ago when I really needed you?" Buck grumbled, scratching Skeezix's nose.

"You're a big boy. I thought you could defend yourself against one small boy—"

"And one dog, extralarge?" He patted the side of the bed. "Want to join us? Might as well. I think everyone else is here." He lifted his head. "No, guess not. I don't see Lolly."

Gopher giggled, bounced.

"Gopher! I mean it. Mr. Riley wants to go back to sleep."

"Nope. He don't. I can tell." The bed jiggled.

"Mr. Riley definitely wants to go back to sleep. Mr. Riley, however, is getting up and joining the human race." Lifting his head again, his eyelids finally coming unglued, Buck surveyed the room. "Oh, Lord. Worse than I thought."

"Too much sunshine, Jonas?" Not much sympathy in that scratchy bedroom voice of hers.

"Too much energy, Jess, that's what." He propped his head up with one hand. At least he was making a start. He studied her for a second, waiting for his mind and body to click into gear.

"Not used to waking up with a tornado, huh, Jonas?" Her mouth quivered, and she puffed out her cheeks, reining in laughter. Jessie was taking a shade too much pleasure in his predicament. In spite of her soft eyes and ready compassion, the woman had a streak of mean, she did. "Bachelor life is more sedate, I imagine."

"Bachelor life is very sedate. Very quiet. And very solitary."

"Sorry to hear that, Jonas." Eyes dancing with enjoyment, she clamped her teeth on her bottom lip.

"I can tell. A font of pity, that's what you are this morning, Miz McDonald."

"I try." She moved into the sunlight, blinding him with radiance and well-being.

"By the way, Jess, where did you unearth a garment with that many colors?"

"Like it?" She whirled in front of him, snagged Gopher and Skeezix and dipped away, legs flashing in front of him.

"I can't make up my mind." He blinked. Some kind of skimpy, shapeless piece of apparel almost covered Jessie's essentials. The barely-bigger-than-a-handkerchief material looked like an abstract painting gone out of control. Pink, red, orange, purple. Black. Squiggles and triangles. And spaghetti? He blinked again, focusing his eyes. No. Not spaghetti. Yellow corkscrews. He wasn't sure the corkscrews were an improvement.

And long, long, smooth bare legs that started at the floor and kept on going up, up, and disappearing under that scrap of a dress. Legs that made his toes curl with the pleasure of looking at them. Hell, no question about it. He was wide-awake now. "Do you go out in public in this, Jess?"

"Of course. Why wouldn't I?"

He was tired, but he wasn't stupid. "Of course you do. I can't imagine what I was thinking." Dragging the sheet with him and wrapping himself in it, he sat up. "Come on, Gopher. We'll shave."

At the door, Jessie hesitated. "Jonas, I have to take Gopher over to Lolly's in an hour and then head to work. I'll be back early, though, today. You can find whatever you need in the fridge. Make yourself at home." She shrugged. "More or less. But don't think you have to work on this house all day. That's not necessary, hear?" This time, genuine concern flowed over her. "I mean, I know we joked about trading labor for lunch, so to speak, but it was only joking, right? You've been up all night. You need rest. Sleep. Don't be silly, okay?"

"Yeah," Gopher piped in. "Don't be silly, okay, Mr. Jonas?"

"George Robert, don't be rude." The bedroom voice turned stern, and Jessie's glance at her son wasn't amused.

"Wasn't," he said mutinously, his bottom lip stuck out far enough to trip over. "You said it first. *You* was rude. Not Gopher." He shook his head adamantly. "Uh-uh."

"That's it, George Robert McDon—"

"Gopher, how about digging out my ditty bag from the duffel over there?"

"Yep." Scrunching up his shoulders, Gopher shot him a big-eyed look and galloped for the duffel, tipping it upside down in a flurry of treasure hunting.

Buck hadn't meant to stick his nose in where it clearly didn't belong, but Jess was about to banish the squirt—and with good reason—but Buck had been enjoying the kid's attention. Selfish, probably, but he wanted the kid to stick around a bit longer.

Jessie glared at him.

"I know, I know. But men have to shave, Jess. Even rude men."

"I *told* you. I *wasn't*—" The voice stopped midsentence, and another pair of T.J.'s shoes clunked onto the floor as Gopher realized that silence was the better part of valor.

"Want to send me to my room, Jess?"

"Wish I could," she grumbled, looking from him to Gopher and back again. "Kids."

Buck stood up, tucking the ends of the sheet around his waist and hiking up the rest. The skim of Jessie's gaze over his bare chest left flash fires in its wake, and he knew she watched him the entire time he strode down the hall into the bathroom because a spot right between his shoulder blades itched like crazy. He couldn't resist slowing his stride to a saunter.

Just before he walked into the bathroom with Gopher right by his side and Skeezix doing his best to squeeze in, Buck looked over his shoulder and caught her staring, her mouth tender and slightly curved as she watched them. "See anything you like, Jess?" he drawled.

"Impossible."

"Not necessarily," he said with a grin and ducked behind the door.

Gopher plunked his bottom on the closed commode lid and handed him the ditty bag. "You got shaving cream in here?"

"Yeah." Buck dug out the miniature can. "Here. You can have this one. I have an extra." Shaking up the can, Buck watched in the mirror as Gopher carefully imitated his motions. "Wait. Shake real hard."

Gopher did. He shook himself right off the commode.

"Whoa." Hooking an arm around the kid's middle, Buck hoisted him onto the counter and showed him how to point the nozzle toward his opened palm.

Cream fizzed, spurted, filled Gopher's hand.

"Want some more?"

"Yeah!" Gopher gave the can to Buck, who shook it up and filled the empty hand held nose-high. "I *luuuv* to shave," Gopher crooned, patting cream first on his own face and then on Buck's.

"I can tell."

In the mirror, Gopher had his eyes closed and was slapping cream from his chest to his forehead. His eyes snapped open. "I need a shaver."

Rummaging through the bag, Buck found an old razor and slid out the blade. "See what you can do with this, kid."

In companionable silence Buck wiped his blade carefully over his face. In the mirror, Gopher imitated Buck's every motion, as serious and careful as Buck himself, a boy in the process of learning to become a man.

Buck felt a lump in his throat.

Men passed on the best of themselves to their children in such small, insignificant ways. Hank and T.J. would live forever in their children, in their children's children, in the memories and family stories handed down.

He wouldn't have this. What he knew, what he valued, would end with him.

He'd thought that was what he wanted. The lone wolf, the man who didn't need anyone.

Now, with Jessie's son following his every motion, he

found himself thinking again about the emptiness of his life, about the choices he'd made.

He had everything.

He had nothing.

Gopher kneeled on the counter and stuck his cream-streaked face close to Buck's. "See? We're just alike, me and you," he said with satisfaction. "Right?" Like Buck, he held his razor in his right hand, his head tilted to the same angle.

"Yeah," Buck said slowly, frowning. He stared into the mirror at the two sets of similar blue eyes, eyes as blue as T.J.'s, Hank's, Charlie's, as blue as Bea Tyler's. He reached out and scooped off some of the cream along Gopher's chin. Rounded, not like his own angular chin, but with that haunting sense of familiarity he hadn't been able to pin down.

From the beginning Jessie's son had seemed familiar to him.

Crazy, the thought that had flashed through his mind.

Impossible.

Like the blue eyes, two matching sets of expressions stared back at him from the mirror.

Reason argued that he was letting his imagination run away with him. Reason told him that what he suspected couldn't possibly be true. He *knew* Gopher *could not be* his son.

But his heart looked in the mirror and told him something else, told him that the impossible could, sometimes, be *possible*.

And wouldn't the heart recognize the truth? Wouldn't a man recognize his own son?

In back of him Jessie's footsteps sounded against the floor as she came down the hall. Then her face appeared in the mirror between his and Gopher's. The three of them, together. Buck regarded her for a long moment, his heart thumping wildly, blood rushing from his brain.

Her hand flew to her throat. "Jonas? Is there a problem?"

"No. Not at all. Right, Gopher? We're finished. Almost," he said around the tightening in his chest. He brushed a clump of dried shaving cream from Gopher's ear, forcing himself to make his motions brisk, uninvolved.

Jessie's son.

His?

His mouth was dry as he smiled, a ghastly smile if the mirror told the truth.

That, of course, was the question.

Was the mirror telling him a truth?

Or was he seeing only what he wanted to see? He only now realized how badly he wanted the mirror's truth to be real. Gopher, *his* son. His and Jessie's.

Caught, he couldn't look away from the mirror, couldn't look away from Gopher, from Jessie as he said, "Gosh, Jess, I keep looking at Gopher and thinking how much he reminds me of someone. Funny, huh?"

Her eyes grew enormous as she stared back at him, and a hint of hurt glimmered out at him. He felt as if he'd slapped her. And then she clasped her hands together, meeting his mirrored gaze. "Really? How interesting. Come on, Gopher. Time to go to Aunt Lolly's."

With a towel she wiped Gopher's face free of cream, her gestures jerky and uncoordinated. She didn't meet Buck's eyes again as she hustled Gopher out of the bathroom.

Buck's hands shook as he leaned against the counter, thinking. Beard-speckled shaving cream dotted the sink. Slowly, slowly, like a man half-awake, he ran his palm around the sink bowl, rinsed the specks of hair and shaving cream down the drain.

Jessie couldn't have kept a secret like that from him. She *wouldn't* have. Straight and true, everything on the table, that was his Jess.

But he couldn't forget the secrets shimmering in her eyes, the wariness behind her fearless approach to life, to him, the way she kept her feelings hidden, protected.

Would the woman he'd known, the woman he thought he knew now—could that woman have kept his son hidden from him? That was a level of deception he couldn't begin to understand. Not now, not with the memory of Gopher's trusting face smiling up at him.

Buck looked at the speck of hair on his finger, then lifted his head to meet his grim, mirrored face staring back at him.

Had it been himself he'd seen in Gopher's reflection?

It was possible. Gopher was four and a half, not four as he'd thought.

The timing was right.

What else could explain her reaction to him, the changes in her life?

In the backwash of anger and pain, he silenced the voice of the advocate, the voice that said there were always, always, at least five sides to everything. *Nothing* was ever what it seemed.

Maybe he didn't have Jessie McDonald figured out as well as he thought he did.

All those unanswered questions that had snaked through his consciousness. She'd never satisfactorily explained why she'd changed careers, turned her life a hundred and eighty degrees around. He'd returned from his leave of absence, she'd disappeared, life had gone on.

And he hadn't forgotten her. Unexamined, locked away in a closet filled with memories, that night had rested on a dusty shelf. Until he'd run into her at the Palmetto Mart.

Turning on the faucet, he let the rusty-colored water spurt into the sink. Of course, the whole firm had been undergoing changes at that point. He'd looked for her, but he'd had no reason to believe that her disappearance had anything to do with him. With that one night.

He smacked his hand against the faucet, cutting off the spray.

By God, he was going to ferret out the truth, no matter what defenses she threw in front of him. No matter how tough she thought she was, he was tougher. More ruthless. He'd seen her fight, and lose, the battle against her tears. Jessie, on the other hand, hadn't seen half his arsenal. She didn't have a chance against him.

If she thought for one damned second that she could keep his son, his *child* away from him, she'd learn what a real battle was.

Anger spurted through him, and he was glad she wasn't anywhere near him. He wasn't sure he could control his thoughts, his words, and he wasn't ready to lay *his* cards, his suspicions, on the table. He could play a waiting game. Patience was his strength.

Jess might have secrets. But not for much longer.

To find out what he needed to know, he could ignore the crackle of sexual need that sizzled between them. He wadded the damp towel in one fist. Or, he could use the sizzle for his own ends.

And he would forget that glint of pain in her eyes.

If she'd kept his son from him, she deserved whatever pain she brought on herself. Because he would never, ever, have walked away from her, from his child.

That was unforgivable.

Wiping the counter and sink dry, he strolled out to join Jessie and Gopher. She was sitting there, as innocent as Eve before the apple, and he didn't trust her for a second, not with what he suspected, not with that suspicion becoming certainty the longer he stared at her and Gopher. She'd denied him his son.

Pulling out a chair next to Gopher's, Buck said, "Listen, Jess, just a thought, but why don't you let Gopher stay with me today instead of going over to Lolly's?"

Gopher popped out of his seat and leaped onto Jessie's lap. "Oh, please, please, please? You're my beautiful mommy and I love you and you love me and you want me to be happy and I'll be *sooooo* happy if you let me—"

"Take a breath, Gopher," Jessie advised, unmoved by the model-wide smile of her son.

"But—"

"Yeah, Jess, why won't—"

"Whoa, fellas." Puzzled, she scanned Jonas's casually helpful expression. Something was wrong. "Give me a second to think this through, will you?"

"Of course. Whatever works for you. For Gopher." Jonas leaned back, apparently indifferent to her decision.

But he wasn't. Despite the negligent drape of his elegant hand over his chair, despite the ear-popping yawn and charming "sorry," Jonas Buckminster wasn't as uninterested in her decision as he appeared. He was on the hunt.

"Yeah, whatever works." Gopher smiled beatifically at her. "Me and Mr. Jonas could work. And me and Auntie Lolly don't do that."

"What's up?" She addressed her question to Jonas. "You need to rest, you might be going in to the hospital. Why would you want to tie yourself down to the house and my son—" She stopped.

His face had sharpened, the angles and planes suddenly tough-looking and not at all indifferent. "I'm not going to the hospital until this evening, Jess," he said, and the contrast of that mild voice with those gunfighter-intense eyes sent chills down her spine.

Chapter Nine

Jonas stayed.

With Jessie hot on his tail trying to catch him, Gopher leaped out of his bed each morning and tumbled on top of Jonas, waking him up. A sleek, bare-chested, sleepy-eyed Jonas Riley in a welter of bedclothes did nothing for Jessie's peace of mind or her dreams.

And he knew, he *knew*, damn him, *exactly* what the sight of him did to her. Oh, sure, pride made her pretend otherwise, but he was no fool. His slight smile was as good as a registered letter.

The first day, she'd hurried home to find Gopher and Jonas painting the living room. Boxes had been shifted to the high-ceilinged dining room and the floor was plastic-draped. The windows were open to air out the paint fumes, and in the ninety-five-degree heat, the room was stifling hot. Jonas's T-shirt was plastered with sweat to his spine, his rib cage, and as she walked in, he lifted the bottom of it to wipe the sweat off his face. His shiny-wet abdomen glistened above the low-slung metal snap of his jeans and a drop of sweat trickled down his smooth chest toward the tidy indentation of his navel.

Jessie couldn't take her eyes off the slow slide of that drop as it followed the lines of muscled flesh and finally slipped under the waistband of his jeans.

He didn't even smile. If he had, she could have joked, turned the intensity of the moment aside. But he simply stood there, the paint-spattered cotton of his T-shirt wadded in his hand, his skin all bare and shiny. Then, as if he, too, had been caught in a spell, he frowned, let the shirt fall into place and snagged Gopher as he barreled past the full paint tray, lifting her son up and swinging him into her arms.

Jonas's expression was haunted, but she didn't have time to think about it, not with Gopher's paint-laden fingers patting her cheek. Returning his excited greeting, she let him down and turned in a circle, really seeing the changes in the room.

"Hey, there, Jess. You look like something the cat dragged in. Hard day, huh?" Jonas smiled at her, a slow, teasing smile that melted her aching bones and turned her insides to jelly.

"Kind of." She sank onto a plastic-covered chair that crackled and rubbed against the backs of her legs, a folded point snagging her nylons.

As Jessie collapsed onto the sticky hot plastic, Lolly walked into the room from the kitchen. She, too, had a paintbrush in hand. Spattered with creamy white, the three of them reminded her of gleeful ghosts.

"I was lonesome, Jess, so I came to give Jonas and George a helping hand. I brought lunch and stayed. Hope you don't mind?" Lolly looked sheepish. "They were having so much fun."

"Fun?" Jessie regarded her with exasperation. "Lolly, I *told* you—"

"Now don't fuss at me, Jessie. You'll ruin everything. We've had our very own painting party."

From his squatting position near a paint can, Gopher smiled up at her. "With mango cobbler and hot dogs."

"And chips," Jonas added seriously. "Lolly brought home-made chips."

"It was no problem, really. I fried them early this morning. Before it got so hot."

"Oh." Jessie didn't know what to say. A painting party. Looking at the three people in front of her and sniffing the smell of fresh paint, she wished she'd been with them. She felt left out, as if everybody in the class had been invited to a birthday party except for her.

"Don't be sad, Jess. We saved a piece of the cobbler for you." Jonas tapped her nose with the end of his paintbrush.

The cool paint actually felt good. She rubbed her nose. "I see. Good thing you did."

"And I think Skeezix, who, by the way, is in the backyard only because he kept tipping paint over, might have spared you a chip. Maybe. If you're lucky. Are you feeling—lucky, Jess?"

Did everything he say have double meanings, or was she succumbing to heat and paint fumes? "I'm always lucky, Jonas," she replied without looking at him, choosing instead to draw Gopher close to her as he tried to skip across the plastic in an uncoordinated loping gallop.

"Me too," Jonas said, giving her nose another tap.

Bending over, Lolly popped the lid on the paint can near her. Encased in bright blue, new denim, her narrow rear end caught Jessie's eyes. Lolly didn't wear jeans.

"Nice britches, Lolly," Jessie said.

"I think so, too. I got to thinking about what you said the other day, and I decided my life needed shaking up. I hit that shop at the mall. You know, the one where all the teenagers buy their blue jeans?"

Amused, Jessie could only nod.

"These fit."

Jonas laughed. "And a fine figure of a woman you are, too, Miss Lolly."

"Oh, shush, you silly man. I'm too old to go out in public like this, but," she said, patting the rear of her jeans complacently, "I'm thinking I don't look half-bad." She waggled her paintbrush in Jonas's direction. "And don't you say a word."

"Wouldn't dream of it." Jonas made a zipping line across his mouth, but his eyes flashed with humor and his easy, hip-shot stance was all confident male.

Jessie's heart turned over. She could have fallen in love with him in that moment if—

Lolly interrupted her thoughts. "My grandson's coming for a visit in about fifteen minutes, Jessie, and I promised him I'd steal George if you didn't mind. Okay?"

"Gopher?" Jessie gestured vaguely in his direction. "What do you think, love bug?"

"Want to go." One streak of paint bisected his chest.

"Okay, then." Nodding, she said, "Whew. I can't believe the work y'all did. This is incredible."

The walls had been sanded, picture holes spackled and the recessed lighting fixture she'd bought had been installed along one wall. The room would be gorgeous, bright, clean, spacious.

"We aim to please, Jess." The gleam in his eyes told her how much and exactly how he'd like to please, and it had nothing at all to do with painting but everything to do with a dark room and the two of them, alone.

"Hmm. Well, yes. No."

"Nothing to say, Jess?" His eyes laughed at her. "That's real unusual."

Gopher and Lolly handed her their paintbrushes and left.

In desperation, she fled, mumbling after her, "Let me have a minute to change, and I'll help finish in here."

She didn't miss the painting party after all. They painted silently, side by side for a few minutes, their feet making crackling noises against the plastic as they shifted positions. She asked for an update on his father. Nothing was new. As the minutes passed in a haze of heat and paint fumes, sweat popped out along her ribs and her forehead, dripped down her back.

With the paint roller in one hand, Jonas clasped her shoulders and turned her to him. "You're an advertisement for spontaneous combustion, Jess. Hold still," he added as she jerked back. Lifting his shirt, he wiped her face.

She inhaled deeply, drawing in the scent of him mixed with paint. Reaching out to steady herself as he dragged the cloth over her neck, she touched the slick skin of his stomach, her

palm sliding down the damp skin. Against her neck, Jonas's
hand stilled, the hem of his shirt brushing her suddenly aching
mouth.

Moving her hand in small circles over his stomach, feeling
the tremors under his skin as she touched him, Jessie found
her breath coming faster and sharper as she pressed her fingers
into his taut skin. "Jonas," she whispered, "kiss me. Please."
The question came from a place inside her she hadn't ac-
knowledged for years, and the need and the wanting were
more than she could endure. "Please," she said in a small,
frightened voice, afraid he'd reject her, think her too aggressive. No sooner had the thought flashed through her mind than
she was backing up, pushing away.

But he dropped the paint roller and snugged his arms around
her, pulling her smack against his sleek, bare stomach. Distantly she heard the wet, plopping sound of the roller as it hit
the plastic. The late-afternoon heat pressed against them,
moved through them until she didn't know whether the heat
came from outside, inside. Fused to him, she sculpted the long,
lean line of his back, let her hands speak of the beauty of his
muscles and bones, let her touch tell him how much she
wanted his touch, let her mouth melt under his, let her tongue
touch his, shyly, as though she'd never kissed before.

And then, roughly, he groaned. "Jess," he muttered into
her ear and lifted her into his arms. His tongue traced the curve
of her ear, sending cold shivers over her, as he stumbled
against the plastic sheeting on the floor and carried her with
him to the plastic-draped sofa in the middle of the room, collapsing with her in a mad crackling and popping of plastic.

His hands measured themselves along her rib cage, his
thumb smoothing the bottom edge of her bra, slipping under
to the tender, sensitive skin. "I remember you like this." The
edge of his thumb brushed her breast, quivered deep inside
her to her womb. "You do, don't you, Jess?"

"Yes," she breathed, flattening his palm against her and
struggling to slow the rainstorm patter of her heart that left
her dizzy with need.

"You like this, too." His thumb brushed her nipple and she

went rigid with pleasure, dissolving in a shower of sparkling colors behind her eyelids.

"Oh, yes." She twisted against him, wanting to be closer to the heat blasting from him, craving his touch. Her foot skidded against the sticky plastic, stuck. "And you, Jonas? What do you like?"

"Everything, Jess. Anything."

Inexperienced, she didn't know where to touch, where to press. She ran the tips of her fingernails along his spine and his shiver answered for him, his touch turned urgent, wilder, his palms cupping her bare breasts and tugging at her nipples until her toes curled and she jolted against him, lost in a haze of heat and pleasure and all of it coming from Jonas.

"I can make you feel good, can't I, Jess?"

"Yes," she answered, scarcely knowing she was speaking. "I love— Oh, yes, there, Jonas. Please."

His laugh was low, a rasp over her collarbone as he nudged her legs apart. "There, sweetheart?"

"Hmm." He'd been her first, her only, lover. The first time she'd been too caught up in the wonder and the glory of the moment, in the rightness of the moment. Now, though, she was old enough to know how special he was, how much pleasure touching her gave him. Turning to him, she wrapped her arms tightly around his waist and sighed. Past, present and Jonas in her arms, his mouth hard and hot against hers.

"Look at me, Jess." Passion mingled with something perilously close to anger in his voice, and she opened her eyes, let them fill with the fierce blue blaze of his. "Who do you see?"

All embarrassment fled in the face of his stark question. His face was strained, his eyes narrowed with need and that emotion that resembled anger. She reached up to stroke his eyebrows. "Me. You." Running her fingers through his hair, she added, "Us, Jonas."

"And you like what we're doing, don't you? You like my hands on you, don't you, Jess?" Again, that disturbing undertone that made her stir restlessly against him. Plastic popped beneath her as she moved closer to him.

She edged one hand under the back of his T-shirt and scraped her fingernails lightly along his spine, delighting in the shiver of his body over hers. "Yes, Jonas, I like this. I like it as much as you like my touch against you." Her eyelids fluttered shut.

Clasping her fanny, he slid her up against him, anchored her against him with a leg thrown over her shorts-clad one. The denim of his jeans scraped her inner thigh and she shuddered with pleasure, with need, with all that she felt for this complicated, vulnerable man whose very touch could make her forget everything except him.

And her son.

She'd told Jonas she wouldn't go to bed with him.

She'd insisted she couldn't, shouldn't, wouldn't.

She wasn't prepared to make love, to have sex, with Jonas. Gopher and Lolly could return anytime.

And, finally, there was that hint of anger, as though he resented her—or himself—for what they were doing. As though he were trying to prove something to himself, to answer some question she couldn't hear and he could.

As fast as water rushing down the drain, she went cold and still. Something was wrong.

She opened her eyes and saw his face looming above her. Too close, too strange in the aftermath of all that heat. She pushed him away, drew her knees together, up to her chest. "I don't want to do this, Jonas," she said tightly. "I made a mistake."

"Was it a mistake the first time?" His knuckle caressed the side of her throat. "Why did you make love with me then, Jess?"

Hiding her face, she rested her head on her knees. "I told you. I wanted to. Tonight I don't want to."

"Just a momentary fling? Is that all that night meant to you, Jess?" His palm cupped her neck and he wove his fingers into her hair, tugging until she lifted her head and faced him. "Nothing more?"

She shook her head free of his grip and met his challenging

gaze, not understanding the intensity in his question. "I told you. Once, twice. I forget. Nothing more, Jonas."

"You're lying, sweetheart. You should see how dark your eyes turn when you do. It's a giveaway every time. Once you know what to watch for."

"According to you." She smiled. "But, Jonas, once in a while, you make a mistake, you know. Not often, I'll admit, but the possibility is there."

"Really?" His tone was wryly mocking. He ran his thumb over her cheek down to the top of her shirt, eased aside one button, his eyes never leaving hers. "Well, then, sweet Jess, why, after all those years of *not* wanting, why did you suddenly change your mind on that lovely spring night?"

"It wasn't sudden," she said through clenched teeth.

"No? How interesting." And then he leaned over and kissed her, his mouth warm and firm against her skin in the gap of button and buttonhole. "I'm off to the hospital, Jess. We'll talk another time."

"I don't think so," she muttered to his departing back.

"I heard you, Jess." His about-face was so quick that she gulped audibly. "And, yes, we will have that talk. I think it's time we *really* put our cards on the table."

The door clicked quietly behind him, leaving her open-mouthed and jittery.

During the next three days, she felt as though she were being herded down an ever-narrowing tunnel toward some corral where an unpleasant end waited. She wasn't sure what it was about Jonas's attitude that made her uneasy, but he watched her, studied her, as if he were waiting for—for *something*. If she'd had it to spare, she would have bet a thousand dollars that he had some agenda of his own in mind, but she couldn't figure out what it could possibly be.

He *crowded* her. He made her aware of him with every movement of his body, with every word he spoke. She knew the touches were deliberate. He wanted her. The way he hesitated a beat too long before stepping back, before dropping his hand from her shoulder, told her there was nothing accidental in the brushes of his body against hers.

And in his eyes was the unspoken recognition that she wanted him, too.

What continued to disturb her was the occasional simmer of anger she glimpsed like storm clouds way back in his blue eyes. She still couldn't decide whether or not the anger was directed at her or himself, but it was unsettling.

Twice she almost told him it was time for him to leave, find another place. She didn't. Taking him aside to tell him privately what she'd decided, she ended up talking about the work he was doing on her house. The words she wanted to say lodged in her throat.

Even unsettled as she was, Jessie wasn't sure why she hesitated. She knew at least ten polite and twenty semipolite ways to tell him the situation wasn't working.

The plain truth was, though, that the situation *was* working for everyone except her. She was the one who was becoming increasingly uncomfortable. She was the one who was giving a pretty darned good imitation of a woman sitting on a red anthill, waiting for the fiery sting.

Jonas seemed remarkably content spending time with Gopher, Gopher, of course, was as happy as a pig wallowing in mud, and Lolly had found a friend from her church group to go to square dances with. The house was being repaired dirt-cheap.

On edge and tired, Jessie splashed water over a cheese-crusted baking dish. Even with the money she'd allotted for repairs and emergencies, she couldn't have afforded all the work Jonas had done. He was fast, thorough and he had a knack for finding a way for Gopher to help. Jonas didn't make busywork for her son, either. The jobs he organized for Gopher were legitimately useful. With a low-key, "hand me the Phillips screwdriver, kid" approach, Jonas was teaching her son.

Everything was peachy-swell. Scraping browned cheese off the glass with her fingernail, she tried to ignore the sounds of hammering and giggles coming from the porch. Jonas and Gopher had torn down one of the porch columns and were replacing it.

"Big mess. Termites ated it, but we got rid of them, Mommy," Gopher had advised her the day before, a pencil stuck behind his ear wobbling as he nodded his head sagely. "Gotta take care of rotted wood and stuff or the house will fall down around our ears."

Standing behind Gopher, one hand resting lightly on the boy's head, Jonas had kept his narrowed gaze on her, making her shift her feet, twitch and fidget as she listened to the child and watched the man.

She heard the echo of Jonas's calm voice in the way Gopher imparted his nugget of information, saw Jonas's lean elegance in the way Gopher tried to keep his chubby hands tucked into his jeans' pockets. Her son, her dog, even Lolly, who'd succumbed to Jonas's courtly flirtation, all adored the man.

Oh, everything was really swell, it was. Jessie flicked soap bubbles across the narrow width of the stainless-steel sink. So what the heck was the matter with her?

She was crazy, that's all there was to it. She had to be imagining that undefined sense of threat coming from Jonas, that quickly hidden anger. After being a single parent, a basically nondating parent, for so long, she must be confusing the emotions running between them with something else. Maybe she was seeing desire and misreading it as anger.

Could the sense of being threatened come from her own uncomfortable mix of emotions where Jonas was concerned, a bubbling, roiling soup of shared history, sex, and— Lifting the dripping dish out of the suds, she glowered at its rainbow-shiny surface. Anger and desire were both hot emotions. She'd confused the two. That had to be the explanation.

Even as she played devil's advocate, she didn't buy her own argument for a minute.

As for Jonas's father, Jonas kept his nightly vigil, the stress showing in the dark shadows under his eyes and in the grooves on either side of his mouth. He was grieving for his father and keeping everything inside.

She knew, though, that his simmer of anger didn't come from Hoyt Tyler's illness. Jonas's anger felt personal. He might believe he was keeping it under control and hidden, but it was directed toward her.

Sloshing water thoughtfully back and forth, Jessie decided she didn't like waiting around for answers. She didn't like feeling as if she were under a microscope. His anger didn't scare her for a second, but he owed her an explanation. She didn't like playing teeny-tiny mouse to his very sharp-toothed cat. If Jonas wanted to settle a score with her, he could. But she was going to decide the time and place, not him.

The kitchen door rattled back on its hinges, and the two males strode in, one set of chubby, short legs hopping two to one in order to keep up with the longer, muscular ones. "Done," Gopher announced as he tried to chin himself on the kitchen sink counter beside her. "Me and Mr. Jonas is going shopping tomorrow. I need shoes and he needs—" Feet knocked against the bottom drawer. Gopher hung, arms crossed, from the sink. He turned to Jonas, who stood in the frame of the door. "Whatcha need, Mr. Jonas?"

"Everything." Jonas filled the kitchen with his presence, and Jessie's skin prickled all over. "You name it, I need it." Once more there was that disturbing note in his voice.

"What?" The dish wobbled in her hand, and before she realized it, Jonas had taken it from her.

"Careful."

"I try to be." She plunged her shaking hands into the sink and grabbed the scouring pad. She could make an innuendo or two of her own. "When's Hoyt going home, Jonas?"

"Tomorrow." He placed the dish on the counter and leaned his hip against it, penning her in between the angle of the cabinet and the sink, Gopher hanging between them.

"Really?" Flipping her braid out of her way with a soapy hand, she glanced up at him. She must have been wrong. Bea Tyler had been wrong, too. Hoyt was going to be all right. Relief welled up in her. "That's terrific."

Jonas was silent, his gaze fixed on the toes of his boots.

"Isn't it?" Worry nibbled at the edges of her uneasiness, and for the moment she ignored the thickening of the air between them in a greater concern.

Jonas lifted his head and met her eyes briefly before saying, "Gopher, would you mind getting that hammer I left out on the porch and bringing it in for me? Thanks."

"Yeah." Gopher's shoes smacked against the floor. The door opened, slammed.

Taking a step, Jonas reached around her waist, grabbed the dish towel and swiped at the glistening baking dish.

She pressed close to the sink, avoiding even the most minute touch, yet the air heated around her, hummed, and her ears were ringing with the rush of blood through her body. Unexplained anger aside, no wonder she felt threatened. All Jonas had to do was step into the room and her skin tightened, hummed, buzzed.

All of which she could have ignored. She knew she could have. She'd ignored those tingles years before. Until the Chapman case verdict came in. That night she'd made a different choice. She'd yielded to the mix of desire and concern and want.

Gritting her teeth, Jessie squirted more bright green soap into the water. She'd told him she didn't regret that night, and she'd meant it. But she didn't want to repeat it. The risks were way too high. She'd just have to watch herself, that's all. She *could* disregard the way her body responded to this cowboy with a carpenter's apron tied around his narrow waist and his scruffy boots planted too close to her own feet. She knew she could.

Except that she worried about him.

That she should worry about six-foot-plus Jonas Riley who could do anything he set his mind and will to was the most amazing fact of all to her.

And she liked him.

She liked watching him with her son, liked watching Gopher's unconscious imitations of Jonas's speech and actions.

After convincing herself all these years that she and Gopher were doing quite well all on their own, she was discovering that she'd been wrong. Clearly Gopher had yearned for a role model with a deeper voice and bigger muscles. Unfortunately he'd picked Jonas Buckminster Riley, a man who could have no part in their lives.

Jessie rinsed soap off the heavy cast-iron skillet and handed it to him. He took it, and his palm shimmy-slid against her wrist. Then, leaving shivers in his wake, he reached to his left and placed the skillet on the burner.

"Your father?" she reminded him tentatively.

Gas flame swooshed out, blue-white, as he fiddled with the stove knob and glanced at her. "Most of the test results are in. They're not good."

"Oh, Jonas," she whispered and clasped his hard hand between her wet ones. "I'm so sorry. What's happening?"

"I called the hospital while you were at Lolly's with the dogs. Daddy's coming home. Then we wait for the bone marrow test and one more CT scan. After that, we'll conference with his doctors. We'll know exactly what we're facing within the week."

Her hand hurt where he gripped it. "I'm sorry, sorry," she repeated helplessly, holding on to him.

"Me too." He stared for a moment at their joined hands, not meeting her eyes. "I didn't want Gopher to hear."

"No," she agreed. "He wouldn't understand."

Jonas's laugh was harsh. "Hell, *I* don't understand. He's a good man, Jess. He doesn't deserve any of what's happening. Neither does Mama." He shook his head as if he'd been hit. "Neither does that little girl. What's her name? Kelly Marie. She's how old? Two? Three?"

"Four and a half. Gopher's age. They were in the same preschool group for a while. Before they found her leukemia." She bowed her head. "I see her, and I think how lucky, how blessed I am, and I come home and try to forget how guilty I feel every time I kiss and hug my son." She rubbed her hands together, hard. "I try never to forget how lucky I am."

"I can understand that."

She pulled the plug on the sink. Water gurgled noisily down the drain and, her head bent over the sink, Jessie watched the last of the soapy water slip away. A lot of things of value could slip away that easily, that unremarkably, she thought.

For minutes, she stood like that, thinking of Kelly Marie and sending up silent prayers for her, for Hoyt Tyler, and for all the others who passed however briefly through the doors of the hospital and the VA center, through her life.

"Will she be all right?" Resting his weight lightly against her, Jonas draped his arms over her shoulders.

"What?" She jumped. His arms skated down her back, over her hips, something almost affectionate in the casual touch. Flipping her braid out of the way, she leaned back into the corner of the sink and cabinet, creating space between herself and Jonas. If she plunged into an affair with him, would she then be immune to the fizz of his every touch? It was a thought. A shade of indifference would be a welcome change, restful. "What did you say?"

"Kelly. How's she doing?" Buck hadn't intended to ask that question. Easier not to know, not to think about the small girl. He didn't want to carry the weight of that knowledge, but the child was Gopher's age. The child in that hospital bed could be his son. That knowledge blasted past his defenses. He folded the dish towel carefully and handed it to Jessie.

She clenched it between two tight fists. "We're waiting to see if she's in remission after the chemo. The expectation is that she's going to need a bone marrow transplant, and they'd like to do it as soon as they can find a match. She doesn't have any brothers or sisters. Even if she did, she'd have only a thirty to thirty-five percent chance. Unless she came from an exceptionally large family. Then the odds would go up. Her family's hoping to find a match." Her voice shook, but her eyes were dry. "Wouldn't you think that out of over thirty countries and over two million potential donors, they could find one compatible donor for a little girl?"

"Yeah." He lifted the weight of Jessie's braid, curled the silky tail of it around his finger. His heart ached for Kelly Marie, for her mother and father and the unending weight of their love. "She's so young. Can they even do a transplant at her age?"

"Two-month-old babies have them. Kelly sure can." Reminding him of Kelly's hold on Skeezix, Jessie wove her fists in and out of the dish towel. "If the chemotherapy can achieve another remission. If the remission holds long enough for a donor to be found. If, if, if." She tossed the towel aside with a quick motion that revealed her feelings about Kelly Marie more clearly than words would have. *"If."*

He understood *if.* "And if all that happens?"

Jessie's smile knocked him out of his boots. "Why then, Kelly gets a miracle. She'll be cured. At least there's a thirty to forty percent chance she will be."

He thought of Kelly's steroid-induced round face, her thin arms and legs, thought about the fears she must have, the terror her parents lived with every day. Thirty to forty percent. Three kids out of ten. Maybe four. "Scary odds."

Jessie nodded once, hard, a desperate emphasis, he thought, in the the fierce movement. "But better than zero. Those odds give her hope. Anyway, I don't want to talk about Kelly. Not now, not after hearing about your dad." She rubbed her forehead. "Choose a subject, Jonas."

"All right." He tugged her hand down from her forehead and held it, his thumb absently circling the mound at the base of hers as he spoke. If he ever needed a champion, he'd want Jessie on his side. She was a ferocious fighter.

Struck, he stilled the easy movement of his hand over her neck, her shoulders. He was becoming altogether too accustomed to having Jessie beside him. Her cheeky refusal to give him a pass on anything tickled him, lifted his melancholy thoughts about his father.

He couldn't remember the instant it had happened, but the scent and feel of her were becoming as necessary to him as the air he breathed. If she weren't around, he went looking for her, needing to see her, needing to hear the husky voice zinging back at him. Taking a deep, shaky breath of that air filled with her Jessie-scent, filling himself with her, Buck realized he had a problem bigger than trying to find out why she wouldn't tell him that Gopher was his son, too.

"Change the subject, huh?" Shifting closer to her, he worked his thumbs into the tight muscle running across her shoulders and delighted in the unconscious way she sighed and leaned toward him even though he knew she didn't want to.

"Oh, yes. I could use a more cheerful mind-set, Jonas."

The tail of her braid slipped over his arm, and he lifted the smooth, silky rope and skimmed it along the edge of her chin, watching with narrowed eyes the way her skin rippled, shivered. Ah, Jessie, he wanted to say, what a wonder you are.

But he didn't. She owed him explanations. He would have them.

"A cheerful topic? Let me think." His words slowed down as he worked his way through his thoughts and his hands across her shoulders and back. "Ah. What would you say about going to the Fourth of July rodeo with me tomorrow? I'm sponsoring a couple of guys from my spread and T.J. and Hank each paid the entry fee to ride. Mama insists she's not leaving the hospital until Daddy walks out with her, but Daddy wants us to go. 'Don't keep fussing over me,' were, in fact, his exact words. Gopher would have a hell of a time. The other kids are going, too. And," he added, allowing himself the indulgence of stroking the long blue vein along her neck, "it would be a change of scenery. You might enjoy it, too. Kinda sweaty and sticky. Buggy." He let his thumb linger in the pulsing base of her throat. Her unconscious response, the arch of her neck and the helpless flutter of her eyelashes, gave him exquisite pleasure.

"Buggy?" Her voice drifted into silence. "I'm not crazy about mosquitoes."

"I have skeeter spray. I'll take care of you."

She went still, her body stiffening under his hands. "I can take care of myself."

"So you keep reminding me, Jess." He skimmed the back of his knuckle along the small bumps of her spine, ending up in the bare spot between shirt and shorts. "I'm only offering a can of bug spray. Probably wouldn't kill you to accept it, you know."

"Probably not." She angled her head up at him and laughed. "But with you, Jonas, I'm never sure."

"Smart lady." He stepped back, his boots creaking against the floorboards.

"As I said, I try to be careful. Even about little things." Her voice carried a warning that had nothing to do with bug spray.

"Me too, Jess. Didn't one of the saints say something about God being in the details? Well, sweetheart—" he leaned over and kissed her, taking her soft, full mouth in a brief, hard kiss that left him craving more even as he thought of her duplicity "—so am I. I'm real careful with the little things in life."

Chapter Ten

The rodeo was hot, crowded, dusty. And buggy.

Buck was grateful for age and the maturity to realize he didn't have to haul his rear end up on the Brahma bulls and wild horses anymore. Still, there was that moment when Jessie's eyes went wide and her mouth fell open as she watched Hank climb aboard his mount that made Buck momentarily rethink the advantages of maturity. He'd switched Gopher to his left arm, keeping the boy close. Jessie had laughed up at them, looked away from Hank, and linked her arm through Buck's arm that held Gopher, making a circle of the three of them. She'd lifted up Gopher's shirt, kissing the boy on the belly, and Buck's heart had skipped a beat. He didn't envy his brothers.

He had Jessie.

He had his own son.

Gopher attracted dirt and sticky candy like a magnet. Jessie whipped out a box of wet towelettes or something along that nature and cleaned Gopher up. Again and again, until just before twilight she pitched the box into the trash and shrugged. "Why do I bother?"

"Boys like dirt."

"Yeah," Gopher chirped, patting the top of Buck's head enthusiastically. "Dirt!"

"It's part of our nature," Buck said solemnly, giving himself over to the playfulness of the day. In the dimming light, kids were flicking sparklers back and forth, the lights echoing the happiness bubbling inside him. "We're hopeless."

"Good thing women have a strong urge to redeem and redecorate, then." She'd hip-bumped him and skipped backward teasingly in front of him and Gopher.

Buck thought she reminded him of one of those fabled will-o'-the-wisps, elusive, flitting ahead, almost out of sight. He'd let her skip away too often. He couldn't lose her again.

She'd come back into his life, and he wanted to keep her there. To keep his son there. She and Gopher filled the emptiness inside him. All the unfocused loneliness found an answer in her, in the child, and the restless, dissatisfied cravings found their answer in her smile, in the touch of Gopher's chubby hand around his neck.

"Down," Gopher demanded. "Want to walk in my boots."

Buck swung him down, Jessie snagged his hand and, swinging at the end of both of their arms, Gopher kicked a clump of dried-out weeds very satisfactorily.

"Men," Jessie said, rolling her eyes and laughing. Even in the twilight, he could see the pink tip of her nose, the sun-flush kiss along her cheeks.

"But you *luuuv* me," Gopher crowed, pulling away from her grip and dangling in Buck's. "You *luuuv* me."

"Now why would I love you, you grubby imp?" Jessie chased Gopher, who dodged around Buck.

"Because I'm your boy, that's why! You gotta!"

"Darn," she said, laughing up at Buck. "He's right."

And in that laughing instant when the world hung suspended in twilight and Fourth of July sparkles, Buck's whole world shifted, righted itself.

Then Gopher shouted "Can't catch me!" and Jessie took off after him, her hair flying free of the flag-patterned scarf anchoring her ponytail. The scarf fluttered to the ground.

"Oh, damn," she said. "George Robert! You stop! Right this minute!"

Maybe it was the urgency in that muttered imprecation, maybe it was the speed with which Gopher barreled toward the fence separating the bulls from the milling crowd, but Buck leaped after her, passed her.

Roaring with laughter at the sight of the two grown-ups chasing him, Gopher scuttled up the wooden planks of the pen and dropped onto the other side, into the show arena.

"Aw, hell." Heart pounding with dread, Buck vaulted after him, Gopher's shirt slipping through his grasp. It was one of the worst moments of his life. He knew if they all lived safely through the next seconds, he would never, ever forget the sight of Gopher trotting toward the middle of the arena where the bull rider had just charged out of the holding pen.

Dust plumes rose in the glare of the spotlights. The ground shook with the force of thousands of pounds of whirling, twisting beast thundering against it.

"Jonas! Oh, Jonas, please!" Jessie's scream came clearly to him over the roar of the crowd and the blare of the tinny speakers announcing the rider's name and times.

Then a moment of absolute peace and silence enveloped him, everything slowing down, the huge bull hanging in midair, his horns hooked to the side, and Buck lunged, grabbed Gopher and rolled to the fence, rolling, rolling, while the ground shook underneath him and Gopher chortled into his neck.

The rodeo clowns in their barrel outfits dashed by, distracting the bull. Over the loudspeaker the announcer led the crowd in cheers.

"Hey, Mr. Jonas." Gopher's blue eyes stared up at him. "Can we do that again?"

"Don't think so," Buck said gravely, wrapping the boy tightly in his arms and struggling to his feet. His knees had turned to liquid. Shaking, he hooked an arm over the arena fence boards and pulled himself up and over, into safety.

Dust choking him, his son in his arms, he headed for Jessie and a showdown.

He'd almost lost this wiry, wiggling lump that was his child, almost lost him and never known him.

Grim-faced, Buck strode toward her. He'd given Jessie as much time as he could. He needed answers. He'd wanted *her* to tell him Gopher was his son, but she wouldn't. Even with Gopher tucked safely in his grasp, Buck hadn't figured out why he wanted her to admit it on her own, but he did. Well, now Ms. Jessie McDonald had run out of her grace period.

"George Robert, you are grounded for the rest of your nat-ural-born life, do you hear me?" Tears streaked the dust on Jessie's face as she reached for Gopher.

"Fun, Mommy! Jonas and me wrestled in the dirt!"

Burying her face into Gopher's neck, Jessie didn't speak, and Buck reined in everything he'd been about to blurt out.

This wasn't the right moment, not with adrenaline pumping through his veins and making him careless. He couldn't con-front Jessie in front of Gopher. Buck shook his head, clearing it. He was going to have to wait after all.

Until they were back at Jessie's house.

The ride back through the purple darkness was silent. Go-pher slept, Jessie leaned against the window and Buck gripped the steering wheel as if it were a lifeline while he made his plans in the aftermath of fear and fury. However things turned out, this night would change his life irrevocably for better or worse. The echo of the old ceremony didn't escape him, and he loosened his death grip on the wheel as an idea came to him.

He'd always had a knack for working the odds in his favor. He could do it again. The stakes were higher than they'd ever been in his life.

They ate a mostly silent supper, making only desultory com-ments. He helped her clean up the kitchen while a chastened Gopher headed to the porch.

With the dishes stored in the dishwasher and the pots and pans washed, Buck planted himself in front of her. He'd never been this nervous in his life, not even the first time he'd argued a case in front of the State Supreme Court. Much more was at stake this time. His life was on the line.

Shutting the drawer with the knives and spatulas, he said, as casually as he could, "Jessie, don't you ever wake up in the night and wonder what would happen to Gopher without you?"

"Not more than every other night, no." She trailed her hand along the counter, moving away from him and toward the porch. "Most single parents live with that really swell nightmare, Jonas." Her hand was on the door. "I worry about him every second I'm awake. About days like this one. About not being able to protect him. Comes with the territory," she said wearily. "What's your point?"

"Jess, slow down and let me ask you something, okay?"

"Sure, whatever. Fire away."

She was utterly exhausted, drained, and he squelched the pity that tempted him to let her off the hook until another time. He could tell she expected him to ask for help with making some kind of arrangements for his father.

"We get along well, don't we?" He waited patiently for her answer.

Talking about Kelly Marie earlier had brought home to him how terrifyingly vulnerable Jessie and Gopher were. And today, well, that had scared him out of ten years of his life. They needed him. Hell, he didn't even know if she could afford the damned pair of shoes he and Gopher were shopping for tomorrow.

Gopher had said he had a budget and he had to pitch in his birthday money if he wanted the shoes with the swoosh. Maybe Jessie was barely making ends meet in spite of her job. He sure didn't want his kid doing without stuff he needed.

There were things a father needed to do for a kid, for his son. Gopher had been without a father for long enough.

"Well? Do we or don't we? Get along pretty well?" He brushed her nose teasingly with the end of her braid, keeping his actions smooth, nonthreatening, lulling her into security.

"I suppose. For two people who tend to argue for the fun of it."

"Yeah. We do argue." He shrugged and dropped her braid. "But only because we enjoy the sparks. Right?"

The raised eyebrow was the only confirmation he was going to get.

"Let me throw an idea out for you to think about, okay?"

"Be my guest. But then, in a way, you already are, I suppose. What's your proposition, Jonas?"

"Simple, really. We're real good together, Jess. Physically. Right?"

She bit her lip and glared at him. "I guess so."

"Guess? Shame on you, Jess." He gave her a quick grin. "Anyway, we're interested in the same things."

Nodding and backing away from him, she watched him warily.

"So why don't we get married?"

"Now there's a dumb idea." She turned her back and walked out onto the porch, her head and spine rigid.

"Not so dumb, Jess." Jonas had followed her onto the porch and stood in front of her, blocking her way to her son.

At the far end of the porch, out of hearing distance, Gopher had built a fortress out of porch cushions and was playing in it.

The sudden tension leaping out of nowhere made Jessie want to run back inside as Jonas unwound the end of her braid and threaded his fingers through the strands, his touch gentle, soothing, contrasting with the flare of his nostrils, the tight line of his mouth as he slipped his hands into her hair.

"Very dumb, Jonas," she repeated, keeping her tone light as she mercilessly squashed the yearning leaping up inside her. In the moment when she'd seen him rolling across the dusty arena with her son, she'd seen her life ending, and then Jonas had given her back her son, given her back her life, and now he was handing her happily-ever-after on a silver platter, everything she'd wanted, and she couldn't reach out and take it.

In a way, she thought, trying so hard to ignore the wistful longing surging through her, it was almost amusing. A tiny part of her, a fragile, hopeful part, whispered, tempted her, told her that maybe he'd discovered after all these years that he loved her. But she knew better than to yield to that honeyed, treacherous voice. "You never wanted to get married, Jonas. Why now?"

He studied her face for a long time, making her uneasy, before he answered her. "Gopher needs a father."

"You're worried about Gopher?"

"Yeah. That's about the size of it."

"How—charitable," she said faintly, stunned. She wanted love, and he offered her a father for her child. All in all, despite the temptation, not a proposition a self-respecting woman could live with. The price of sacrificing her pride would be too high in the long run. Marriage was hard enough. Without love, it would be a soul-killer for her. "That's not your concern, Jonas, is it?" She shaded her eyes as she looked up at him, politely warning him off the subject.

"I think Gopher is my concern."

"What?" Lost, she frowned.

"You couldn't get to him in time today, Jess."

"You're right, and you have to know how grateful I am, but I don't understand what you mean, Gopher is your concern?"

"You know what I'm talking about, Jess. Our son."

"*Our* son?" She staggered, at last comprehending where his complex brain had taken him. She'd known the corral could be deadly. She hadn't had the slightest hint of where he'd been herding her, though, and couldn't have prepared herself in a million years for what he was saying. "You don't know what *you're* talking about, Jonas."

"Your son. Mine. Ours. The son we made five and a half years ago, Jess. That's who I'm talking about."

She grabbed Jonas's arm. "You'd better spell out exactly what you mean because you're making no sense at all." Her heart was going lickety-split. "Gopher is my son. How could you possibly think he was yours?" She shook his arm, terrified. "Remember, we were both—careful that night. Even in the heat of the moment, neither of us took that kind of risk. *Both* of us were—prepared."

He put one hand on either side of her head and leaned in, his face close to hers. "Nothing is foolproof where sex is concerned. Except abstinence. And there was no abstinence that night, was there, sweetheart? Accidents happen all the time."

"There were no accidents, Jonas." She sank onto the floor, her back against the wall. "None," she said dully. "Oh, Jonas, how could you believe that I could—that I could have had a child and never told you? You think I'm that kind of person?"

He hunkered down in front of her, reaching for her hands, but she snatched them away. "Jess, it's all right. I'm crazy about him. I love him. I never wanted kids, and now I'm stunned by how much I love our son."

"What a reassuring statement that is, but, Jonas," she repeated tiredly, knowing there would be no escape, "George is *not* your son."

His face closed against her stubbornly. "Then whose son is he, Jess? I don't know why, lust, a full moon, but you went to bed with *me* that night, no one else. You could never in a hundred years make me believe that you hopped out of my bed into someone else's. Nothing could make me believe that."

"*Ergo,* George is your son?"

This time he captured her hands and held them tightly, not letting her withdraw them. "Yes. Nothing else makes sense."

"How kind of you. To give me credit for sufficient discrimination to keep from leaping merrily from bed to bed, especially in this day and age. Thank you, Jonas, I can't tell you how touched I am by your trust." Sarcasm sharpened her tone. "But to believe that I'd *lie* about having your child? I'm not quite sure which view is more insulting, Jonas, if you want to know the truth."

"Why is the truth insulting, Jess? I don't understand. Help me out, here, will you?" Seductive, gentle, that voice filled her ears.

Jessie stared down the porch at her son. She didn't know how much more she could take. The whole day with its roller coaster of delight and fear and now Jonas was going to strip all her secrets from her and leave her with no pride, no defenses, and she didn't know how to stop him. "You're treating me like a hostile witness, Jonas. Why?'' she wailed softly, her emotions finally spilling free. ''Leave it alone, please!''

''I can't.''

''No, I suppose you can't. I wish you could believe me.'' She bit her lip to stop the trembling. He was going to make her tell him everything she'd shoved into that closet for years.

''Talk to me, Jess. Tell me what the truth is, then, because in my heart I *know* he's mine. I can't believe anything else.''

''That's what all this is about? The marriage proposal? The carefully orchestrated seduction over these past few days? You want to marry me because you think my son is yours?'' She pulled herself to her feet, needing to be upright, no matter what. ''Let me make sure I have the whole picture. You never wanted to get married, never wanted a child, but now that you think you have a son, you're offering me marriage, even though you think the mother of your son, the woman to whom you're so generously offering your hand in marriage, you think that woman, me, is a liar—and a thief?''

''You're not a thief, Jess.''

''Really?''

He shook his head.

She refused to let him see how hard she was shaking. Her world was flying apart in little pieces and she wanted to grab all the shiny pieces and save them for the long nights ahead, all those nights when she'd lie awake regretting this moment with every cell in her aching body, with every beat of her lonely heart. ''But according to you, I stole your child from you. That makes me a thief, no matter how you try to white-wash it.''

''I want my son, Jess.''

A killing cold was slowing down her blood, numbing her. ''Is that what this is all about, Jonas?'' He'd never wanted *her*, only her body. And now he wanted her son, the child he seemed to believe was his, and to get his child, he'd take her. ''Sort of a two-for-the-price-of-one?'' She was appalled.

''You and I, Jess, we have something special together. And I want to make up to my son for all the time I've lost. I want him with me, Jess. I intend to see that he is. One way or another.''

''Your biological clock isn't my concern, Jonas. Just because you suddenly decide that you like the idea of being a father doesn't mean you get to be an instant dad. Fathers are guys who're there every day—''

''I would have been. If you'd given me the chance.'' He sighed. ''Jess, why not make it easy on all of us? Tell me the truth. We can work everything out. I think the logical answer is for us to get married, but we can figure out the details later.'' He gripped her arms, holding her in place.

She sagged, her knees buckling, but she stayed upright. She would see this through to the end, and then she'd lick her wounds in private. ''All right, Jonas. You wanted the truth. Here it is. I went to bed with you that night because I'd been in love with you from the first week I went to work at Collins, Keane and Riley.''

''You were in love with me?'' His frown was thoughtful, surprised. ''That's why you slept with me?''

''For whatever macho satisfaction that gives you, Jonas, yes.''

''I don't take that kind of pleasure, Jess. You know that. But I wish— Well. I never guessed you felt that way.''

''You weren't meant to. My feelings were private. Mine.''

''That was the night the Chapman verdict came in. I was miserable, filled with self-disgust, and I went to the office looking for someone to talk to. I found you.''

She nodded and tried to keep her head from repeating the motion over and over. ''You found me. You walked in looking as though you'd just killed someone, even though you'd just won the biggest case of your career, a precedent-setting case. No one else was in the office, and I couldn't bear watching your misery. It broke my heart.'' She swallowed the tiny sob creeping into her throat.

''Ah, I see.'' He stepped away, freeing her. ''Charity on your part, Jess, the offering up of the sacrificial virgin?''

''No. I gave you the only comfort I could. I wanted to be with you.''

"I hated myself that night, Jess. Hated the law, hated my life. I'd argued brilliantly on behalf of my client. I won, but I was praying that I'd lose. I wanted to lose, but I was too competitive to figure out a legal way to lose. Harold Chapman was a murderer and I was the reason he walked out of that courthouse a free man instead of in cuffs. And he was the reason I never practiced law again." His forehead rested against the flaking paint of the porch, and he rolled his head back and forth. "I hated myself and you saved me."

"You did what you were supposed to, Jonas. You gave him the best defense you could. That was your job." Even in her anger, she gave him this truth. Because she remembered too well the desolation, the turmoil in his face that night.

He held up a hand, stopping her as she started to walk away. "One thing, Jess. Gopher has my eyes, he looks like the kids in my family, and everything I know tells me he *has* to be mine. Unless Gopher was some sort of immaculate conception, how do you explain that he's not?"

"You won't leave me anything, will you, Jonas?" Jessie gathered her courage and faced him. "You're right. I would never have gone to bed with someone else after that night we spent together. I loved you. That was reason enough for me. I'd never expected to fall in love, and I tumbled head over heels in love with you. Like everyone else." Her laugh rose wildly, a raw sound even to her own ears. "Oh, I guess we practiced safe sex, but the irony is that I didn't practice safe *emotion*. I had no idea what I would feel. Being with you was all I wanted. It was enough."

Unbearably moved by her declaration, Buck almost reached out to take her in his arms. Her pale face was distant and beautiful, and he wanted her more than he'd ever wanted anything in his life. He was only now beginning to understand the maelstrom of emotions and confused motives that had brought him to her. "I'm honored, Jess. That you feel that way. That you let me be your first lover."

Something stirred in her eyes.

He blinked. "What is it, Jess? I don't understand."

"Gopher?" she called.

The boy looked their way, started to rise. "Don't want to go to bed yet. I like this Fourth of July."

"No, love bug. It's not bedtime. Jonas and I are going to look at the garden. We'll be right back." She opened the screen door and stepped onto the newly repaired stoop, letting the door swing gently shut behind her.

Right behind her, Buck caught the door and shut it. The door still needed some work. He'd have to fix— His hand lingered against the new plastic screen. He probably wouldn't be here tomorrow.

The yard was dusty dry in spite of the rains. Patches were visible where Skeezix and the other dogs had dug past grass to dirt. Buck wondered how far away from the house and into the dark Jessie was going to lead him. At the edge of the fence that separated her house from Lolly's, she stopped, sinking down onto an old pine log that bordered a wild stand of hollyhocks that provided shade during the day from the blast of the late-afternoon sun. He could barely see her face in the dark. In back of them, from the house, the light glowed, a rich yellow spilling into the night.

"Jonas, I think you were more accurate than you realized when you joked about your biological clock. I think you want a change in your life so badly that you've convinced yourself that my son is yours. Please believe me that he's not. If he were, I would have told you at the beginning."

"I believe you, Jess." With the dry smell of earth and flowers around him and the memory of that look in her eyes, he felt his certainty ebbing. "But I still want you to tell me."

"I was—attacked."

"What?" Her words made no sense to him. Raped? Not Jessie.

"Three weeks after you left." Jessie's voice was flat, unemotional, that of a woman reciting a grocery list, perhaps.

With her first word, Buck wished he'd backed off, never tried to wear her down until she'd tell him what he needed to know. Jessie was dredging up a memory that had almost destroyed her, and her pain sliced through him. Not that she was a drama queen. No, just the opposite. He wanted to protect her from this memory and he couldn't. It was his fault she was reliving this. "Who?"

She dug her feet into the dirt. "Who doesn't matter."

"'Who' always matters." Watching her small toes work their way into the dirt, Buck could have killed the man who'd hurt her. For all Jessie's sturdiness and back-at-you demeanor, she was vulnerable, fragile. And someone had used her brutally. Unforgivably. "Who did that to you, sweetheart?" He kneeled in the dirt in front of her and lifted her feet onto his thighs, balancing them there and folding his hands around their small, grubby nakedness. Too late the protection, the care, but it was all he could do.

"Jack," she whispered in a voice as empty and dry as the dirt.

"Jack Keane?" His friend, his partner, his childhood buddy?

"I was alone. At the office. Jack came back to—pick up some papers." Her face was vacant, smoothed free of emotion as she recited. "I thought he didn't know I was there. For all these years I exempted him from planning what he did. I thought he acted on the spur of the moment. But you said—" Her eyes met Buck's, but he didn't think she really saw him, not lost in the past as she was. "You said that everyone knew I worked late at night. I suppose he planned what he did. Somehow that makes it worse." Her shoulders shook once, but then she sat as straight as a young girl in pioneer times with a board strapped to her back.

"It's okay, sweetheart," he murmured, stroking her feet, rubbing them, and dying a little inside with each word. "I wish I could kill him—"

"Too late."

"I know."

"Afterward, when he was done," Jessie sobbed, but not a tear fell from her empty, staring eyes, eyes that looked right through him to the past, "then he begged me not to say anything. If I did, his life would be ruined. His wife was my friend. He had three children. He *begged* me, Jonas—" She lifted her hands, let them fall. "And then he left."

"So you didn't report him?" Buck couldn't imagine the Jessie he'd known back then not going immediately to the police.

"I sat there at my desk for hours. Betty Lou was my friend," she repeated. "I didn't want to hurt her. To hurt those three children."

"Aw, Jess." Buck leaned forward and lifted her onto his lap, switching positions so that he was on the pine log. "Jack was a clever, devious man and a hell of a lawyer to have on your side. He boxed you in. He *knew* what he was doing."

"I finally figured that out. But, Jonas," she said, resting her face against his chest, "I was so *ashamed* and humiliated!"

"It wasn't your fault. You didn't do anything to cause him to attack you, Jess. It wasn't your fault."

"I know. I knew, even then, up here." She tapped her head. "But here—" she moved her hand to her heart "—*here*, that was different. I knew him, you see. We'd worked together. I'd been to their house for *dinner*, Jonas! In their home where his children were! I didn't move for hours. I couldn't. And then I knew that I had to call the police. I couldn't let him do to someone else what he'd done to me, could I?"

"No, sweetheart. And he would have. I heard stories about Jack, but I dismissed them. I thought people were jealous of him. He was the kind of guy to inspire jealousy." He smoothed her hair back from her face, trying to kill the fury beating like the wings of a captive bird inside him, kill it the way he wanted to kill a man long dead. "No one ever said anything when I returned for that week before I sold out my share of the partnership."

The leaves of the hollyhocks and sunflowers stirred in a passing breeze. Jessie's skin was clammy, even in the heat. "No one knew. The police came when I called. The female detective took me to the hospital. While we were there—" Jessie's voice faltered for the first time "—while we were there, she had a call. Jack's car had gone off the abutment on the bridge to the island. They said he'd been drinking. He hadn't. At least not when he—"

"And you let the report die?"

"Yes." A whisper of sound, that admission.

"And you found out later that you were pregnant."

"Much, much later. Four months later. I was so thin and I lost even more weight, afterward—" She sobbed again, that tiny, wounded cry that had no tears and pierced his soul. "And I couldn't stay at the firm. I couldn't go into my office—"

That was where it had happened, then. No wonder she'd left. "It was a power play. It had nothing to do with sex, Jessie, nothing to do with you as a woman. It was raw power, and Jack used it. But you were stronger than he was. You reported him. He would have paid. In the end, you won."

"I didn't care about winning." She rubbed his shirt between her fingers. "I only wanted to be able to do what I loved, to work, to look people in the eyes and not wonder if they knew my dirty little secret and blamed me for what happened." Tears leaked from the corners of her eyes down her cheeks. "I wanted my *pride* back. That's what he took. That's what hurt the most. That he stripped me of my pride and self-respect."

"Shh, Jessie. I'm here. You're okay."

"I didn't know I was expecting until almost four months into the pregnancy." She lifted her head and her eyes were clear. "Like you, I never wanted children. I never wanted marriage or to fall in love, and I didn't plan any of what's happened, but it's right for me. I can't imagine life without my son. He came into it and made sense out of the ugliness, gave me a purpose when I didn't have one." Tears shimmered at the edges of her lashes.

"I don't understand, Jessie."

"I love him, you see. None of what happened was his fault. He's himself. I had to get over my anger, or I would have ruined his life and, finally, I came to understand that. Why should my child have to pay when he was as much a victim as I was? How could I teach him to love himself if I surrounded him with hate?"

Pulling her close to him, Buck cradled her against him in the darkness. Such a small frame to bear so much pain so bravely.

Chapter Eleven

Jessie wanted to scream.

For four days Jonas had been treating her as if she were porcelain that the slightest breath would shatter. For a man who didn't tiptoe around anything, she thought he was spending an awful lot of time on tippytoe. Every evening he sat with her on the porch, holding her hand, touching her lightly, briefly, but not touching her intimately, not kissing her.

And every evening he repeated his proposition.

Even Gopher, with his new shoes on, had joined in the act.

And every evening she turned Jonas down. She wanted his heart and he was offering her protection, security. He offered Gopher the security net of a father, and that almost broke her down.

"I can't."

"Why not?" His finger skimmed along the back of her neck. "I'd be a good father. I've had practice with the nephews and nieces. And, besides, Jess, I *want* to be a father."

"I won't have you looking at my son and seeing the past in every feature of his face. I won't risk him."

"I wouldn't do that, Jess."

"No? Can you love him? For himself? Or would you always see Jack Keane's face when you looked at Gopher and think of what he'd done?'' She spread her hands, helpless to make him see that her son's happiness was more important than even the promise of her own. ''I saw your face, Jonas. You would have killed Keane if you could have.''

''For what he did to you? In a minute. In a heartbeat.''

''Then how can you expect me to think you can forget and love my son the way he deserves to be loved?'' With her arms clasped around her knees, she rocked back and forth on the chaise longue. ''I can't marry you. I can't, I can't.'' But she wanted to. For the sake of having his touch, his kiss, for having *him* in her life, in her bed next to her during the long nights, she was ready to risk her heart, her pride.

But not her son.

Jonas gathered the weight of her hair in his hands, lifted the mass so that the evening breeze whispered across her neck. ''Jess, think about this. I believed with all my heart, my soul, that Gopher was mine. Believing that, I loved him, wanted him in my life. That hasn't changed. Love doesn't vanish overnight. I still love him. I want to give him the kind of love my daddy gave me. Biology doesn't make a father. I can be a father to Gopher. I want both of you. You were right. It's a package deal, and I'd be getting the bargain of my life.''

''I can't,'' she moaned as his warm hand cupped her neck.

''Can't, Jess? Or won't?''

''Both.''

''What can I do to convince you?'' His thigh burned against her bare one where her skirt had hiked up as he'd scooted her closer. ''What do I have to say? I can support you both, you know. I'm not the destitute you thought I was. Good grief, Jess, I've made enough money on the stock market to support five families. If I had to.''

Her laugh was watery. ''I'm thrilled for you. The way you dressed, I thought you were next to starving.''

''Well, I'm not. Look, I know you don't need anyone to support you. You've saved money of your own. You're reasonably comfortable, Jess, but think of what I can give Gopher. A family. Cousins. Brothers and sisters. If you're willing, if you'll trust me. Can't you do that, sweetheart?'' His hand cupped her knee, stayed there, didn't stray a centimeter higher.

That final question stopped her. Could she? Could he be the father Gopher needed? The husband she wanted? Could she take the biggest risk of her life? She slipped her finger through the buttonhole of his shirt, his brother's shirt.

Later she would think it was that moment, that careful restraint that decided her, that gave her the courage to reach out for the brass ring. ''Jonas, maybe I could. I believe you love my son, that you could love him as if he were yours. But I need to be sure in my heart that you do. I need time.'' She needed time to decide, too, if she could marry a man who cared for her, desired her, but who didn't love her the way she loved him.

''Take as much time as you need, Jess. I'm not going anywhere.''

''What about your ranch? Don't you have to take care of business back in Okeechobee?''

''Sweetheart, you don't have a clue about my circumstances, do you?'' He fingered the hole over his knee. ''I have a family I pay to run the ranch. I go there for peace of mind, for the sense of doing something worthwhile in life. And recently I've been thinking I'd like to try my hand at a few law cases again, *pro bono*, for people who could use my help. I can afford to use my time that way. That was part of my discontent. I loved being a lawyer, and it killed a part of my soul to leave it. You've made me see that I can still do what I love. But I need you around, I need you to keep me grounded, to keep me from becoming too full of myself.'' He leaned over her. ''I have a tendency to be a shade arrogant and overconfident if I'm not kept in line, Jess.''

''Really? I hadn't noticed.'' She'd worked the button loose without even realizing it.

''I need *you*, Jess, more than I ever thought I needed anyone in my life. Give us a chance.''

His sleek chest was hot to her touch and his heart thundered against her palm, and she shut her eyes and leaped into the void, leaped with faith and hope and love. "All right, Jonas. I'll marry you."

And so, stilling her doubts, she did.

Because Hoyt's release from the hospital had been delayed, they decided to make a small, private ceremony. So, quietly, with no family present except Gopher, Jessie pledged herself to the man she'd loved all her adult life—the man she'd loved enough once to risk herself with—pledged herself now to the man who in every way proved that she could trust him with her child.

In a tiny corner of her heart, she hoped that this man would come to love her a tenth as much as she loved him.

On the day Hoyt came home from the hospital, the Tylers and the Rileys held a combination welcome home/wedding reception party. In the shade of the oak tree on the lawn, Hoyt, thin and drawn and in a wheelchair, surveyed his family. The Tyler twins played ring-around-Grampa and made Hoyt smile with their barely walking antics. Gracie, Hank and Jilly's daughter, had draped herself over the armrest and smiled sweetly up at Grampa. Gopher rested his chin on the other armrest as though he'd always been a part of this family. Hoyt's hand rested on her son's head, reminding her of the casual touches Jonas passed out so easily to Gopher, who'd abandoned her for this tall male in his life.

Watching the melee, Jessie smiled, too. All the noise, the confusion, the richness of this family washed over her, making her and Gopher a part of them. Not wanting it, not even knowing this richness was what she needed, she'd found it, a blessing she'd never expected.

Her son would be blanketed and supported by the warmth and caring of all these people, his life enriched in a way she could never have planned. Her own small contribution to family, Lolly, had brought her own friend, an elegantly dressed gentleman who'd been a lawyer, too, and the couple wandered among the throng of Tylers.

She tucked her arm in Jonas's and walked with him toward his father. "He looks good, Jonas, considering. He's fighting."

"Yeah." Jonas gripped her hand so tightly that her wedding band cut into the flesh. "He is. Maybe, like Kelly Marie, he'll get a miracle, too."

"Hi, Hoyt," Jessie said, kneeling next to his chair and putting her hand over his pale one. Buck stood in back of his father, shading him.

"Hey there, yourself, Miss Jess." Hoyt curled his hand around hers, the same way Jonas did, that protective, masculine grip reassuring.

Jessie swallowed past the sudden lump in her throat. "This is a beautiful day, isn't it?"

Hoyt tipped his face to the sky, bright, bright above them, and the sun gilded the gray of his face, burnished it with warmth. "Sugar, every day is beautiful." He smiled, and Jessie could see the reflection of his sons' killer smiles in the appreciative grin he gave her. Resting his head against the back of the chair, he said, "Buck, how about taking a walk and letting me visit with Jessie a while?"

"Sure, Daddy. Come on, monsters." He motioned to Gopher and Gracie, who trailed noisily after him, competing for his attention.

"You love my boy, don't you, Miss Jess?" Now, with only the two of them present, Jessie heard the tiredness, the exhaustion.

"To distraction."

"Good." A shadow passed over Hoyt's face. "He's going to need you, need your love, Miss Jess. It makes my heart easy that he found you. I've worried most about Buck. Funny how it turned out that he was always kind of my favorite, you know, being my first, even though he wasn't mine by blood. But it felt like he was. The other boys, well, they have someone of their own. Buck didn't. And now he has you and your boy. He won't be alone. I'm glad."

Jessie swallowed past the lump in her throat and whispered, "I'm glad, too."

"He loves you, you know."

"I'm not sure." A weight lifted off her shoulders as she confessed her fear to this man with his wise, tired eyes.

"He can't take his eyes off you. Every time you move out of sight, he ambles over until he's near you." Hoyt patted her hand. "He loves you, Miss Jess. Don't ever doubt it." His eyes shut, and his hand rested, paper-thin against hers.

Jonas came up behind her, kneeled down beside her and, like Gopher, rested his chin on his father's armrest. Jonas took Jessie's free hand in his. "I heard what you said, Jess. You didn't know I loved you?"

"No," she whispered, hearing the truth in the sigh of the breeze, seeing the love she hadn't recognized blazing back at her from Jonas's eyes.

"Why the hell did you think I wanted to marry you, woman?" His murmured voice carried the force of a roar.

"Because of Gopher?"

"Aw, Jess." He bent over and took her mouth in the sweetest kiss he'd ever given her. "Don't start selling yourself short. I'm crazy about you, sweetheart."

"Good, son. You should be." Hoyt coughed, leaned back. "And you better take good care of her because I like her."

"Believe me, I will." Jonas gave her a sly smile, letting her know exactly how well he'd take care of her later.

"Bad boy," Jessie murmured to him.

"Oh, I can be very, very good, Jess. Trust me."

She did. Giving him a quick, surreptitious kiss of her own, she rested her head against him, letting the miracle of the day seep into her.

Gopher somersaulted into her lap, squirmed into Jonas's, and Jessie fought back tears of happiness. Her son. Her husband, with the man who'd been his father in everything save blood. And now Jonas was going to be a father to Gopher. The sins of the fathers didn't have to be visited on the sons. Redemption. Salvation. Love.

Looking around her, she took in the wonder of all these people loving each other. Her *family*.

In the distance, Gracie and Charlie, T.J. and Callie's son, were chasing Nicholas, their cousin-by-marriage-and-by-adoption.

Jessie wondered if she'd ever get all the relationships straightened out.

She would learn. She had time.

They all did.

Hoyt was a fighter. And he was surrounded by such love that it took Jessie's breath away, leaving her astonished.

Winter and darkness were a long way off.

In the meantime, they had all summer, all these golden days ahead of them stretching out before them, all this richness of time and love.

And miracles were always possible.

*   *   *   *   *

Afterword

This book is dedicated with immense affection and appreciation to some saints and angels at Loyola University Cancer Center:

Dr. Ellen Gaynor and Dr. Patrick J. Stiff: You do an impossible job with kindness and humanity. You may not win every battle, but you fight the good fight. And every year you even the odds. Bless you.

The members of the Bone Marrow Transplant Team and Dr. Maholtra, who keeps us in stitches—one way or the other!

The oncology nurses who've been there day in and day out since the beginning with incredible kindness and patience: Mary Rotolo, Anita Brown, Michelle Crebo, Pam Schumacker, Elena Callas, Louise Reedy, Chris Quirch, Jennifer Schmoldt. Thanks, too, to Laura Kinch, Shari Lichtenstein, Liz Taylor and Marianne La Croix, who help keep everything on keel.

There's not enough gold in the world to reimburse all of you for what you do, for what you've done. In a just world, though, there would be. Thank you for encouragement, information and laughs—even on rainy days!

Silhouette's newest series

YOURS TRULY

Love when you least expect it.

Where the written word plays a vital role in uniting
couples—you're guaranteed a fun and exciting read
every time!

Look for Marie Ferrarella's upcoming Yours Truly,
Traci on the Spot, in March 1997.

Here's a special sneak preview....

1

Morgan Brigham slowly set down his coffee cup on the kitchen table and stared at the comic strip in the center of his paper. It was nestled in among approximately twenty others that were spread out across two pages. But this was the only one he made a point of reading faithfully each morning at breakfast.

This was the only one that mirrored *her* life.

He read each panel twice, as if he couldn't trust his own eyes. But he could. It was there, in black and white.

Morgan folded the paper slowly, thoughtfully, his mind not on his task. So Traci was getting engaged.

The realization gnawed at the lining of his stomach. He hadn't a clue as to why.

He had even less of a clue why he did what he did next.

Abandoning his coffee, now cool, and the newspaper, and ignoring the fact that this was going to make him late for the office, Morgan went to get a sheet of stationery from the den.

He didn't have much time.

Traci Richardson stared at the last frame she had just drawn. Debating, she glanced at the creature sprawled out on the kitchen floor.

"What do you think, Jeremiah? Too blunt?"

The dog, part bloodhound, part mutt, idly looked up from his rawhide bone at the sound of his name. Jeremiah gave her a look she felt free to interpret as ambivalent.

"Fine help you are. What if Daniel actually reads this and puts two and two together?"

Not that there was all that much chance that the man who had proposed to her, the very prosperous and busy Dr. Daniel Thane, would actually see the comic strip she drew for a living. Not unless the strip was taped to a bicuspid he was examining. Lately Daniel had gotten so busy he'd stopped reading anything but the morning headlines of the *Times*.

Still, you never knew. "I don't want to hurt his feelings," Traci continued, using Jeremiah as a sounding board. "It's just that Traci is overwhelmed by Donald's proposal and, see, she thinks the ring is going to swallow her up." To prove her point, Traci held up the drawing for the dog to view.

This time, he didn't even bother to lift his head.

Traci stared moodily at the small velvet box on the kitchen counter. It had sat there since Daniel had asked her to marry him last Sunday. Even if Daniel never read her comic strip, he was going to suspect something eventually. The very fact that she hadn't grabbed the ring from his hand and slid it onto her finger should have told him that she had doubts about their union.

Traci sighed. Daniel was a catch by any definition. So what was her problem? She kept waiting to be struck by that sunny ray of happiness. Daniel said he wanted to take care of her, to fulfill her every wish. And he was even willing to let her think about it before she gave him her answer.

Guilt nibbled at her. She should be dancing up and down, not wavering like a weather vane in a gale.

Pronouncing the strip completed, she scribbled her signature in the corner of the last frame and then sighed. Another week's work put to bed. She glanced at the pile of mail on the counter. She'd been bringing it in steadily from the mailbox since Monday, but the stack had gotten no farther than her kitchen. Sorting letters seemed the least heinous of all the annoying chores that faced her.

Traci paused as she noted a long envelope. Morgan Brigham. Why would Morgan be writing to her?

Curious, she tore open the envelope and quickly scanned the short note inside.

Dear Traci,

I'm putting the summerhouse up for sale. Thought you might want to come up and see it one more time before it goes up on the block. Or make a bid for it yourself. If memory serves, you once said you wanted to buy it. Either way, let me know. My number's on the card.

Take care,
Morgan

P.S. Got a kick out of *Traci on the Spot* this week.

Traci folded the letter. He read her strip. She hadn't known that. A feeling of pride silently coaxed a smile to her lips. After a beat, though, the rest of his note seeped into her consciousness. He was selling the house.

The summerhouse. A faded white building with brick trim. Suddenly, memories flooded her mind. Long, lazy afternoons that felt as if they would never end.

Morgan.

She looked at the far wall in the family room. There was a large framed photograph of her and Morgan standing before the summerhouse. Traci and Morgan. Morgan and Traci. Back then, it seemed their lives had been perma-

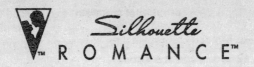

Silhouette
ROMANCE™

COMING NEXT MONTH

#1210 MYSTERY MAN—Diana Palmer
Our 50th Fabulous Father!
Fabulous Father Canton Rourke was in Cancun, Mexico, to relax with his preteen daughter, but damsel-in-distress Janie Curtis was putting an end to that mission. The perky mystery writer was looking for a hero able to steal hearts—would Canton prove the perfect suspect?

#1211 MISS MAXWELL BECOMES A MOM
—Donna Clayton
The Single Daddy Club
Confirmed bachelor Derrick Cheney knew nothing about raising his young godson—but the boy's teacher, pretty Anna Maxwell, was the perfect person to give him daddy lessons. Problem was, she was also giving Derrick ideas to make Miss Maxwell a mom...and his wife.

#1212 MISSING: ONE BRIDE—Alice Sharpe
Surprise Brides
Stop that bride! When groom-to-be Thorn Powell went to track down his runaway fiancée, maid of honor Alexandra Williams reluctantly came along. But as the marriage chase went on, Thorn began wondering if his true bride might be the one riding right beside him....

#1213 REAL MARRIAGE MATERIAL—Jodi O'Donnell
Turning Jeb Albright into a "respectable gentleman" would definitely be a challenge for Southern belle Mariah Duncan. Especially when this strong, rugged Texan had the lovely Mariah thinking he was real marriage material...just the way he was!

#1214 HUSBAND AND WIFE...AGAIN—Robin Wells
Love and marriage? Divorcée Jamie Erickson had once believed in the power of both. Then Stone Johnson, her handsome ex-husband, returned, reawakening memories of the happiness they'd shared, and setting Jamie to wonder if they could be husband and wife...again!

#1215 DADDY FOR HIRE—Joey Light
Jack was glad to help out single mom Abagail with her children. His little girl needed a mommy figure as much as her sons needed a male influence. But Jack soon realized he didn't want to be just a daddy for hire; he wanted the job forever—with Abagail as his wife!

MILLION DOLLAR SWEEPSTAKES
OFFICIAL RULES
NO PURCHASE NECESSARY TO ENTER

1. To enter, follow the directions published. Method of entry may vary. For eligibility, entries must be received no later than March 31, 1998. No liability is assumed for printing errors, lost, late, non-delivered or misdirected entries.

   To determine winners, the sweepstakes numbers assigned to submitted entries will be compared against a list of randomly, preselected prize winning numbers. In the event all prizes are not claimed via the return of prize winning numbers, random drawings will be held from among all other entries received to award unclaimed prizes.

2. Prize winners will be determined no later than June 30, 1998. Selection of winning numbers and random drawings are under the supervision of D. L. Blair, Inc., an independent judging organization whose decisions are final. Limit: one prize to a family or organization. No substitution will be made for any prize, except as offered. Taxes and duties on all prizes are the sole responsibility of winners. Winners will be notified by mail. Odds of winning are determined by the number of eligible entries distributed and received.

3. Sweepstakes open to residents of the U.S. (except Puerto Rico), Canada and Europe who are 18 years of age or older, except employees and immediate family members of Torstar Corp., D. L. Blair, Inc., their affiliates, subsidiaries, and all other agencies, entities, and persons connected with the use, marketing or conduct of this sweepstakes. All applicable laws and regulations apply. Sweepstakes offer void wherever prohibited by law. Any litigation within the province of Quebec respecting the conduct and awarding of a prize in this sweepstakes must be submitted to the Régie des alcools, des courses et des jeux. In order to win a prize, residents of Canada will be required to correctly answer a time-limited arithmetical skill-testing question to be administered by mail.

4. Winners of major prizes (Grand through Fourth) will be obligated to sign and return an Affidavit of Eligibility and Release of Liability within 30 days of notification. In the event of non-compliance within this time period or if a prize is returned as undeliverable, D. L. Blair, Inc. may at its sole discretion, award that prize to an alternate winner. By acceptance of their prize, winners consent to use of their names, photographs or other likeness for purposes of advertising, trade and promotion on behalf of Torstar Corp., its affiliates and subsidiaries, without further compensation unless prohibited by law. Torstar Corp. and D. L. Blair, Inc., their affiliates and subsidiaries are not responsible for errors in printing of sweepstakes and prize winning numbers. In the event a duplication of a prize winning number occurs, a random drawing will be held from among all entries received with that prize winning number to award that prize.

5. This sweepstakes is presented by Torstar Corp., its subsidiaries and affiliates in conjunction with book, merchandise and/or product offerings. The number of prizes to be awarded and their value are as follows: Grand Prize — $1,000,000 (payable at $33,333.33 a year for 30 years); First Prize — $50,000; Second Prize — $10,000; Third Prize — $5,000; 3 Fourth Prizes — $1,000 each; 10 Fifth Prizes — $250 each; 1,000 Sixth Prizes — $10 each. Values of all prizes are in U.S. currency. Prizes in each level will be presented in different creative executions, including various currencies, vehicles, merchandise and travel. Any presentation of a prize level in a currency other than U.S. currency represents an approximate equivalent to the U.S. currency prize for that level, at that time. Prize winners will have the opportunity of selecting any prize offered for that level; however, the actual non U.S. currency equivalent prize if offered and selected, shall be awarded at the exchange rate existing at 3:00 P.M. New York time on March 31, 1998. A travel prize option, if offered and selected by winner, must be completed within 12 months of selection and is subject to: traveling companion(s) completing and returning of a Release of Liability prior to travel; and hotel and flight accommodations availability. For a current list of all prize options offered within prize levels, send a self-addressed, stamped envelope (WA residents need not affix postage) to: MILLION DOLLAR SWEEPSTAKES Prize Options, P.O. Box 4456, Blair, NE 68009-4456, USA.

6. For a list of prize winners (available after July 31, 1998) send a separate, stamped, self-addressed envelope to: MILLION DOLLAR SWEEPSTAKES Winners, P.O. Box 4459, Blair, NE 68009-4459, USA.

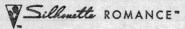

In February, Silhouette Books is proud
to present the sweeping, sensual new novel
by bestselling author

CAIT LONDON

about her unforgettable family—*The Tallchiefs.*

TALLCHIEF
FOR KEEPS

Everyone in Amen Flats, Wyoming, was talking about
Elspeth Tallchief. How she wasn't a thirty-three-year-old
virgin, after all. How she'd been keeping herself warm at
night all these years with a couple of secrets. And now one
of those secrets had walked right into town, sending
everyone into a frenzy. But Elspeth knew he'd come for
the *other* secret....

"Cait London is an irresistible storyteller..."
—*Romantic Times*

Don't miss TALLCHIEF FOR KEEPS by Cait London, available
at your favorite retail outlet in February from

You're About to Become a *Privileged Woman*

Reap the rewards of fabulous free gifts and benefits with proofs-of-purchase from Silhouette and Harlequin books

Pages & Privileges™

It's our way of thanking you for buying our books at your favorite retail stores.

PROOF OF PURCHASE
SR-PP22
Offer expires March 31, 1997

Harlequin and Silhouette— the most privileged readers in the world!

For more information about Harlequin and Silhouette's PAGES & PRIVILEGES program call the Pages & Privileges Benefits Desk: 1-503-794-2499

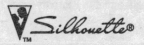

Silhouette®

SR-PP22